W9-APW-156

DEATH IN CANTERA

DEATH IN CANTERA

JOHN D. NESBITT

FIVE STAR
A part of Gale, Cengage Learning

GALE
CENGAGE Learning·

Farmington Hills, Mich • San Francisco • New York • Waterville, Maine
Meriden, Conn • Mason, Ohio • Chicago

GALE
CENGAGE Learning®

LIBRARY OF CONGRESS CATALOGING-IN-PUBLICATION DATA

Names: Nesbitt, John D., author.
Title: Death in Cantera / John D. Nesbitt.
Description: First edition. | Waterville, Maine : Five Star, a part of Gale, Cengage Learning, [2016]
Identifiers: LCCN 2015038001| ISBN 9781432831363 (hardcover) | ISBN 1432831364 (hardcover) | ISBN 9781432831486 (ebook) | ISBN 1432831488 (ebook)
Subjects: | BISAC: FICTION / Mystery & Detective / Historical. | FICTION / Westerns. | GSAFD: Western stories. | Mystery fiction.
Classification: LCC PS3564.E76 D44 2016 | DDC 813/.54—dc23
LC record available at http://lccn.loc.gov/2015038001

First Edition. First Printing: March 2016
Find us on Facebook– https://www.facebook.com/FiveStarCengage
Visit our website– http://www.gale.cengage.com/fivestar/
Contact Five Star™ Publishing at FiveStar@cengage.com

Printed in the United States of America
1 2 3 4 5 6 7 20 19 18 17 16

For J. R., who with his son Ty and their four horses packed my elk out of the timber in the Snowy Range.

CHAPTER ONE

The man named Dunbar came to Cantera in the fall of the year on a cool, cloudy day. I first saw him when I was out with my donkey, Pedro, gathering stones and putting them in the panniers, trying to keep the load balanced. Dunbar came riding down from the north, where a pine ridge with high rock formations ran east and west. I could not see the top of the ridge that day because of the clouds and trailing mists, so Dunbar seemed to materialize, riding a blue roan horse and leading a buckskin that carried his gear.

I thought I should have heard the footfalls of his horses earlier. Maybe the ground was soft and damp from the weather, but a great deal of rock lay about, and some sound should have carried from the two sets of hooves. For a moment I recalled a time, many years earlier in Mexico, when a silent buzzard had floated up out of the mists of a canyon, behind a man who was standing on a broad rock and speaking to me in Spanish. It had been a strange incident, almost mystical, in a faraway place. Dunbar's appearance was not so foreign. I was on the plains of Wyoming, picking up familiar white stones the size of small loaves of bread, and I expected him to speak to me in English. But the overcast day, and the scene isolated by mists, gave the event an unusual atmosphere, and with the rocky background I could imagine the man as an ancient traveler wending his way through a deserted city of stones.

As the rider came closer, I saw that he was a tall man, broad-chested, in a dark, high-crowned hat. He had dark hair and brows and a bushy mustache to match. He wore a charcoal-colored vest, a grey wool shirt, and yellowish leather gloves. He raised a hand in greeting, and a minute later he spoke.

"Good afternoon." His words seemed to echo in the cool air, like sounds coming out of a mist.

"The same to you," I said as I slipped a rock into the pack.

"Havin' any luck?" he said.

"Some," I answered. "This area right here is a good one for these smooth, white stones." I raised a small hand pick that I used for dislodging them. "I suppose some people might take me for a prospector, with my pick and my burro, but I'm more of a gatherer."

"It doesn't look like a prospector's pick. More like a gardener's." As he spoke a longer sentence, he voice sounded normal.

I turned the tool and looked at it. "I suppose it does. At any rate, picking up rocks is not the only thing I do. I just come out here once in a while."

His head moved as he looked over the panniers. "We're not far from Cantera, are we?"

"No," I said. "A couple of miles. On a clear day you can see the town from here." I gazed in that direction. "I'm about ready to go back. If you're not in a hurry, you can poke along with me, but if you want to get there at a better pace, don't mind me."

"I'll poke along. That's as far as I'm going today, anyway." He had dark eyes but a friendly smile. "There's nothing better than a donkey, is there? In its own way, that is."

I looked at my dark pack animal with his large head, long ears, and broad forehead. "He's a good one."

"What's his name?"

"Pedro. And mine's Owen. Owen Gregor." I looked up at the

man on the tall horse.

"Mine's Dunbar," he said. He leaned down and gave me his hand. "Pleased to meet you."

After we shook, I put my pick in the pannier and gave a tug on Pedro's lead rope. As I walked along, I said, "Will you be looking for a place to stay in town?"

"I believe so, assumin' there's a place to be found."

"There are two," I said. "And as chance would have it, one of them is mine. I have a lodging house. You're welcome to stay there. When we get to town, you're free to choose as you please, of course. I wouldn't want you to think I come all the way out here to waylay travelers, under the pretense of gathering stones."

Dunbar laughed. "It would be funny if you did."

"Oh, yes. I'd miss all the travelers coming in on the main road."

"Are there many travelers come through here?"

"Oh," I said with a shrug, "maybe one a month." And so we ambled on, along no road at all, across the plain to Cantera.

In town, Dunbar chose to stay at my lodging house, even though, as I explained to him, I was not in the custom of serving meals on a regular basis. With travelers being few, and at least half of them staying at the boarding house, I hadn't found it practical to keep a supply of food on hand. Dunbar did not seem bothered. As I came to know, he liked conversation, and I believe he chose my place for that amenity, though I think he would have found more variety of talk among the freighters and peddlers who stayed at my competitor's place.

When he had put his horses up at the livery stable and had gotten his evening meal at the Desert Rose Café, Dunbar took a chair in my sitting room. He set his hat on a side table, smoothed his mustache, and let his eyes rest on the little fire I had built. I expected him to take out a pipe, but he didn't.

9

He said, "I understand that this town used to have more going on when the quarries were in operation."

"Yes, it did. When I was growing up, my parents made a good living with this business. But then I went away, and while I was gone, the quarries shut down. I had something to come back to, but not much. I have a roof, and I get by. I even pick up a little work now and then, but I have time to read and time to go out on excursions with Pedro."

"Does he stay here?"

"Yes, I've got a bit of a back yard as well as a shed."

Dunbar laughed. "Back in the old country, they live all under one roof, with the stable attached to the house. Or where they have houses dug into rock, like caves, the animals are in a chamber next door."

"I've heard of that. They say the owners are used to it, but the smell of the animals, especially pigs, is too close for some visitors. I think I'd like a little more distance while I was having my bread and cheese and wine. Or whatever they have in those places."

"I agree," said Dunbar. After a few seconds, he returned to his earlier topic. "Things must have been interesting when the two quarries were in production. There were two, weren't there?"

"That's right. There was the Celeste, or the Frenchman's Quarry, as people call it, south of town, and then there was the Bluestone Quarry to the west."

"A lot of bustle."

"Oh, yes. The Frenchman's Quarry had a rock crusher, ran on steam, and you could hear it from town. And because they mined with explosives, you could hear the blasting as well. There was a railroad spur at the time, so along with everything else you would hear train engines and steam whistles."

"So the town was full of workers, not to mention people who

came and went with the trains and freight wagons and what-
all."

"Sure. And the commerce that lived off of that. Food and dry
goods, clothing, shoes, liquor, tobacco."

Dunbar smiled. "Something like a mining town?"

"Maybe a little," I said. "There were occasional card sharks
come through, and there might have been a few painted ladies,
but we didn't have that kind of a floating population with tent
cabins and all that, like you find in a boom town. Things were
more steady."

Dunbar pursed his lips. "I guess Cantera means quarry."

"That's what I understand," I said. "It can also mean quarried stone. I'm sure you noticed some of the buildings here in
town were made of sandstone."

"I did. It has a good solid look to it. I like it much better
than that yellow brick you see in some places."

"So do I. I've come to appreciate it." I smiled. "Of course,
I've had time to observe it. On certain mornings it's pink with
shades of grey. At noon on sunny days it's a dusty grey, and at
dusk it becomes a kind of parchment color, cloudy, with veins
of blue."

"Maybe I should sit around a few days and observe it for
myself."

"It wouldn't be the worst way to pass the time."

Dunbar raised his eyebrows. "Which quarry did it come
from?"

"All of this in town came from the Bluestone Quarry. Hence
the blue veins. Quite a bit of the stone from there was also
shipped off to a jail that was being built."

"And the Frenchman's Quarry? Was that rock mostly
crushed?"

"Quite a bit of it was, but they also took it out in blocks,
tailored and chiseled into what you think of when you hear of

11

quarried stone."

Dunbar gave a half-smile. "So you have a Frenchman's mine, or quarry, and a town with a Spanish name. What do you make of that?"

I shrugged as I poked at the fire. "It's like other places where you have a Spanish name, but few if any people who live there speak Spanish. Cantera, Moneda, Hermosa. We have a couple of people here who speak Spanish—actually, three that I can think of, but that's it."

"And the Frenchman?"

"Oh, he's dead. Been that way for several years. But his widow speaks French. Or did, when there was someone to speak to."

For all of his questions and interest, Dunbar did not seem impressed by anything I said. It was as if he knew it all before. So I thought I would try him.

"She also happens to be one of the three people who speak Spanish."

"Oh, that's good," he said, still showing no surprise.

"Why do you say that?"

"Well, it's a small town. You like to be able to talk to everyone. And her French probably isn't doing her much good if her husband's dead."

"So is his first wife. And their little boy."

I must have sounded a bit sharp, because he said, "That's too bad. I didn't mean to make light of any of them." He paused. "Or of the town, past or present. I'm sure it had good features at one time, and it no doubt has some left."

"It's not a ghost town, but it's not what it was. I guess that's something we have to accept about the past. When something dies, it's hard to bring it back to life."

Dunbar shrugged as he gazed at the fire. "Not everything dies at once."

"That's true," I said. "You can see that a good part of this town has died along with the quarries, but what's left is hanging on all right. With no other towns for forty miles, people come in from ranches all around. And we do get an occasional traveler, as I said earlier. The railroad is three miles away. There's not a separate town there, or even a station—just a platform and a shack. It's a flag stop."

Dunbar nodded, as if he already knew all of this as well. "I'd like to see a quarry," he said. "That shouldn't be much trouble, should it?"

"Oh, no. Especially the Frenchman's Quarry. There's no one there, and it's not that far away. I could even go out there with you if you wanted."

"That's a good idea. Maybe we'll try it in the morning."

I joined Dunbar for breakfast at the Desert Rose Café. Though he was dressed like a range rider and wore his high-crowned hat and his gunbelt to the table, he did not eat like so many bunkhouse and boarding-house men I had seen. He took his time to enjoy his ham and eggs, and he took interest in doing a neat job of spreading the butter and orange marmalade on his toast. After his comments about the old country the night before, I could imagine him as a traveler in France or Spain, eating his breakfast with leisure at a village inn and then going out to see houses dug into rock mountainsides, or to ponder old monasteries.

As we sat by the window of the café, we could see the bank, a dignified stone building that stood across the street on the north side and caught the morning sunlight. A dark-haired woman went in, and a couple of minutes later she came out and turned to her left.

"Who's that?" Dunbar asked.

"Mrs. Carreau. The Frenchman's widow, as some would say."

"First name?"

"Dolores. Or Doña Dolores, as her hired girl calls her."

"Of course." Dunbar raised his coffee cup. "Do we need to ask her permission to go see the quarry?"

"I wouldn't trouble her. There's nobody there, and it's out in the open. Anyone can ride past it or even through it." I paused as his eyes followed her. "Do you know her?" I asked.

"Not at all." He looked down his bushy mustache at his coffee cup. "But you've made her sound interesting."

"She keeps to herself quite a bit."

"I don't blame her." Dunbar set down his cup. "If I wasn't so inclined to talk and ask questions, I might do the same. Probably should."

Out on the sidewalk after breakfast, Dunbar said he would get a saddle from the livery man and I could ride one of his horses.

"Rent a saddle?" I asked.

He wrinkled his nose. "It's not much."

"I've got one, and a bridle, too. They haven't been used much in the last several years, but they've been stored inside."

"Let's take a look at 'em." He stepped off the sidewalk to cross the street.

When we were halfway across, a familiar figure came out of the bank. As the man looked up and down the street, his badge flashed in the sunlight. His glance rested on us for a second until he turned to his right and walked away.

Dunbar's eyes followed him for a couple of seconds. "Who's that?"

"Pat Roderick. He's the town marshal."

"Must be busy."

"He keeps an eye on things. And he stays up to date by checking in with people like the banker."

"Didn't waste any time on us. Of course, he knows you.

Maybe he thought I was your brother."

I laughed. With Dunbar being above average height and me being below, he was almost a head taller. Add to that his dark, high-crowned hat along with my dust-colored, short-brimmed, battered affair that would do honor to a prospector in the desert, the contrast was more than evident. "Yes, he knows me," I said, "and well enough to know that I don't have any brothers. Or sisters."

"Then this isn't one of those towns where everyone's related."

"Not by blood," I said.

"That's good."

I almost paused in mid-stride. "Why do you say that?"

"Oh, I meant it was a good observation. I'm sure there are people here who are related by blood. Nothing wrong with that. Well, not in the usual sense."

We left town with Dunbar riding the horse he had ridden the day before, the blue roan, while I rode the buckskin. The weather had lifted and the sky was clear, so the country was visible for miles around.

The town of Cantera and the two quarries lay in a kind of borderland where the grazing was sparse and small rocks lay on the surface. To the east, past the railroad, the grassland was better, and so there was a good scattering of ranches, windmills, and herds of cattle. To the north, behind us as we rode, lay the pine ridge that Dunbar had come down the day before. To the west, the treeless plains sloped up toward foothills dotted with cedars and bare boulders. Beyond the foothills, mountains rose up, again with dark cedars and then patches of pine. As the mountains curved away to the southwest, distant buttes rose in a haze. Straight to the south, the country looked flat, but that was an illusion, as the land rolled in dips and rises. A person might see a cow or a horse at two miles away and ride up on an antelope or a cowpuncher a hundred yards off.

La Celeste, or the Frenchman's Quarry, lay south and a little west of town. We crossed the old rail bed of graded dirt and crushed rock, and we arrived at the site. The quarry did not have a spectacular setting that one might expect, such as the rock wall of a canyon or mountainside. Rather, it consisted of a broad hole, not very deep, in a wide, grassy area. One could see where the rock had been taken out of the strata, beginning with a top layer that was a foot to three feet thick around the edges. A few lumps stuck up here and there, looking like headstones, but for the most part, the floor of the quarry was a carpet of smaller pieces that were not usable or that, sooner or later, might have gone into the crusher if it had not been dismantled and carried away. An abandoned work shack and office building sat on a high spot to the east of the large depression.

The place was quiet as a graveyard as we rested our horses. I could imagine the bustle of days gone by, with drillers and blasters, hammers beating on chisels, and the crusher pounding away. Now, only a faint breeze played across the area.

"Why did it go broke?" Dunbar asked.

"It happened while I was away. The main reason, as I understood, was that the two quarries had satisfied all the demand within reasonable distance. What with the cost of extracting the stone and then shipping it, the price was too high for customers very far away—say, Cheyenne or even Denver beyond that. And to tell the truth, I think there was higher quality stone, even if it was farther away, that those customers were willing to pay for."

"And so they shut down, and took away everything of value."

"Pretty much. First the crusher and other heavy equipment, then the rails, then the cross-ties."

"And the Frenchman?"

"He had his own troubles as well. First his wife died. Her

name was Angélique. She was his angel, they said. I remember her, blonde and angelic. He named the mine after her. La Celeste. Celestial, you know. When she died, he married the governess."

"Dolores."

"Yes. She was quite talented. She painted, sang, played the piano. She taught the boy proper French, to tune up what he heard from his father and some of the workmen."

"So she became his stepmother."

"Yes, and then the boy died. A very unfortunate accident. Drowned in a water trough, as I recall."

"That's too bad."

"Yes, it was. I was away at the time, but they say the Frenchman took it very hard. He was a stern fellow as I remember him. He came to the U.S. as a small boy, learned English, and became a relentless businessman. And successful. But his angel died, and then his little prince. At about the same time, the quarry business faltered. He was unforgiving with it all—with his wife, Dolores, with his turn in fortune, and with the world in general. He died very unhappy."

I expected Dunbar to say something sympathetic, but he said, "And the other quarry. I suppose it was something of a rival."

"It was. I think it produced a little bit better building stone, but it had slower production and didn't have a crusher. Still, it did all right until the market thinned out. The owners closed up and went elsewhere."

"And who has it now?"

"The man we saw on the street. Pat Roderick. He acquired it along with a poor-grass ranch—at a pretty good price for him, I think. He calls it the Rock Canyon Ranch."

"And the quarry is the Bluestone."

"Correct."

17

"Does he take any rock out of it?"

"He has taken out a little, I've heard, to build a house, but the progress has been pretty slow."

"So he doesn't do much, if anything, with that quarry."

"No. But whenever there has been talk—and there hasn't been much—of getting this one going again, he seems to get jealous. Says he might start his up again, as well."

Dunbar raised his eyebrows. "Maybe he will. Shall we take a look inside the old building here?"

"Why not? I don't remember ever being inside."

We rode around the edge of the excavation and dismounted in front of the office building. Above the doorway, the words "La Celeste" were still visible in chipped black paint on a white background. Inside, a layer of dust covered the counter, the shelves, the window ledges, and the lintels. Cobwebs hung everywhere, and several of them sagged with dust.

On one wall, just beyond the counter, an old lithograph still held firm, thanks to a dozen dark-headed tacks. I blew off the dust to see it better. It was an antique illustration of a stonecutter with a pointed beard. He wore a round hat with a curled brim, a jerkin with half-sleeves and a waistband, old-fashioned knee breeches, stockings, and low shoes. He was bent over a block of stone, working it with a pointed hammer. At the top of the poster ran the legend *"Le Tailleur de Pierres,"* and at the bottom was a four-line stanza, also in French, stating that there was not a better way to get good stones to build a superb building.

The lettering was archaic, with *s*'s that looked like *f*'s. Dunbar squinted, and I could see he was reading the words and trying to make out the meaning for himself.

On the back wall, affixed with the same kind of dark tacks, hung a lithograph of a stone house. The building consisted of only walls with door and window openings. It had no roof or

18

beams or doors or framed windows. It was titled *"Maison de Pierre."*

"Maison," said Dunbar. "That's French for house, isn't it?"

"Yes, it is. And *pierre* means stone."

"I think I heard that somewhere. By the way, that was the Frenchman's first name, wasn't it?"

"That's right," I said.

"Then that picture is a house of stone, not Pierre's house."

"Correct. And the quaint chap in the other illustration is a shaper or trimmer of stones."

Dunbar glanced at the other picture. "Of course." He came back to me and said, "I thought you said there was only one person in town who spoke French."

"I can read a little, but that's about it."

"I can get just a word or two at a time," he said.

I wondered where he got some of them. To my memory, I had not mentioned that Carreau's first name was Pierre.

When I saw that Dunbar was planning to stay a few days, I offered to serve meals and bought some provisions. That evening I served up a good bachelor's meal of fried potatoes and beefsteak.

"This looks good," he said. "Sorry to see you take business away from the old codger at the Desert Rose, but I believe this is better."

"Horace is all right. I eat there sometimes on my own. But this is more convenient, and it's good for me to stay in practice."

Dunbar stuck his fork in his steak and applied his knife. "No complaints here."

After a couple of minutes of silence, I said, "Just as a matter of conversation, and not meaning to be inquisitive, but are you on the lookout for some kind of business opportunity?"

Dunbar raised his eyebrows and shrugged. "Who isn't on the

lookout? Even your marshal, who must have a comfortable job upholding the law here, has an eye out. Here he's got a ranch, and a quarry to boot."

"As for his being marshal, I don't believe he earns as much as he did when the town was bigger. I doubt that he makes much with his ranch, and I'm sure he doesn't with his quarry."

"Well, you tell me, then. Is there an opportunity here?"

I had to consider. "This is not a prosperous place, but some people do make a living. And for peace and quiet, it's not bad."

Dunbar nodded. "A man could imagine living here if he had an income. I would have my doubts about a harvest of stones, though." He smiled. "Not that there's anything wrong with the activity itself, of course."

"Thank you." I smiled back. "It can be a pleasant pastime in this barren land."

"I might even try it myself, picking up stones. But you know what I mean. To get some kind of production going in a quarry would take capital, and a man would have to rediscover a market. But it's not impossible."

I wondered if he had an actual interest, and if he did, whether his restrained enthusiasm was part of a buyer's strategy.

"How's your steak?" I asked.

"Just fine."

Neither of us spoke for a couple of minutes. To make conversation, I said, "I should have thought to make some biscuits."

He pointed his fork at his plate of meat and potatoes. "This is plenty. Good, too."

"Maybe I'll make some tomorrow."

"Sounds good."

After another minute I said, "Anything I could help you with tomorrow?"

"I don't know. I haven't got the day planned out yet. But at some point I might like to talk to Doña Dolores, as you call her."

"Is that right? Do you think it's a prospect after all?"

"What's that?"

"The business."

"Oh. Well, yes."

"Do you want to bring the Frenchman's Quarry back to life?"

Dunbar tipped his head. "I don't know if I can do that, any more than I can bring back the Frenchman himself." He paused. "I think that what I want, right now, is to know more about this quarry and one or two others."

"One or two? I know of only one other."

He gave me a shrewd look. "There's more than one kind of quarry."

CHAPTER TWO

At breakfast the next morning, I formed an idea of another kind of quarry Dunbar might have meant. I had cooked a meal of bacon, eggs, and fried potatoes, which he was working his way through, and I set a tin plate of hot biscuits in front of him.

"Those look good." He cut one open, spread a dab of butter inside, and closed it. "By the way," he said, in an offhand way, "how's the hunting hereabouts?"

"Hunting? Like deer and antelope? There's not much waterfowl right around here, though the sandhill cranes fly over in big flocks about this time of year, and the geese pass over in November or so."

"I was thinking more like deer and antelope," he said.

"Well, wherever there's grass and sage, there's antelope. For deer you're more likely to find 'em where there's water and cover. So along the creeks, or up in the foothills."

"Either one would be good to try. How do you cook that kind of meat?"

"With antelope, I fry it in bacon grease. With deer, I might fry it or I might cook it in a stew."

"That sounds good. Maybe we could give it a try while I'm looking around at other things."

"We've got a good start. I'll save the bacon grease."

After breakfast, Dunbar put on his hat and went out to check on his horses. I cleaned up the kitchen, and as I checked my supplies, I saw that I would need more coffee before long. So I put on my hat and went out into the sunny morning.

I went to the general store and bought two pounds of coffee. As an afterthought I bought two pounds of dried apples. When I walked outside I was met by Pat Roderick, the marshal. He had his chin raised, his thumbs on his gunbelt, and a general air about him as if he had been waiting for me.

He was in his late forties or early fifties, in good condition, and his clothes fit him well. He had dark hair flecked with grey, plus a mustache of similar color. He kept himself well trimmed, and on this day, as usual, he was clean-shaven. He was a little taller than I was, as well as older, and he knew something of my past, all of which helped him maintain a superior attitude. He lowered his head, bored into me with his brown eyes, and said, "So who's this fella you've got stayin' with you?"

"His name's Dunbar."

Roderick shrugged. "Doesn't mean anything to me."

"Well, you asked who he was."

"So I did. Maybe I could have put it another way. What's he up to?"

"I don't know. He might be looking for a wife."

Roderick gave a brief puff of air through his nose. "Men don't come here for that."

"One thing he mentioned was that he might try his hand at hunting. Men do come for that." I let Roderick wait a few seconds until I added, "And he might be on the lookout for a business prospect. But I don't know."

"Is that why the two of you went to the Frenchman's Quarry yesterday?"

I didn't care for the marshal's insolence in letting me know he kept track of our movements, but I pretended not to notice. "Dunbar was interested in seeing it."

Roderick gave a stronger huff. "That place'll never be worth a nickel."

"It doesn't cost me anything for someone else to look at it."

The marshal's eyes narrowed. "Is that all he's doing—looking?"

"I don't know. You could ask him yourself."

"I don't like his looks."

I couldn't tell if the marshal was making a play on words. I tossed off a shrug. "There's worse-looking men that come to this town and spend a little money in the café, in the saloon, and in one of the two fine lodging houses."

"Well, with some of 'em, you'd better count your change."

"If I buy anything from 'em, I'll do that. There's two ways that money flows in this town, and I'm careful about both."

Our relation seemed to have shifted from that of a lawman leaning on someone of lesser authority to that of a town merchant, however small, addressing a public servant. Roderick's way of not conceding any more was to raise his chin, sniff, and turn away.

I thought, *He didn't like that. He'll find a way to bully me again.*

I wondered if Dunbar had seen any of my exchange with the marshal, for he had a light air about him when he returned to the lodging house.

He said, "The good thing about a day like today is that I'm in no hurry to do anything. I hope you aren't."

"Nothing has risen up and taken me by the throat."

"Good. Then why don't we go to the Desert Rose for pie and coffee?"

I was surprised. Dunbar had not struck me as being that frivolous. I said, "I suppose we could. I just bought some dried apples, and I was thinking of making a pie myself."

He gave a playful frown. "There's nothing to keep you from doing that as well, unless it's the time."

"Oh, no."

"Then let's go. We'll see if the old boy has peach."

Horace was seated at a table in the Desert Rose Café, his head tilted back as he read a newspaper through his spectacles. At the sound of the door he set down his paper and turned to greet us. His grey hair and beard were neat, and his white shirt was clean.

"Well, good mornin'," he said. "What wind brings you here?"

"The winds of fortune. Do you know Mr. Dunbar?"

Horace rose from his chair. "He's been in here. With you, in fact." He turned. "Pleased to meet you. I'm Horace Collins."

"Likewise."

After they shook, Horace turned to me and said, "What fortune?"

"The possible good fortune that you might have some peach pie to go along with a cup of coffee."

"I do. Have a seat."

Horace had our order served within a couple of minutes. He stood by, with his back to the counter where he sold candy and tobacco. In a clear, steady voice that was not a codger's at all, he said, "Are you enjoying your visit to our town, Mr. Dunbar?"

"Yes, I am."

"Something of a shadow of its former self, but some of us like it anyway."

Dunbar cut a triangle off of his piece of pie, looked up, and smiled. "Some of us like shadows."

"We went out to the Frenchman's Quarry yesterday," I said.

"Oh, yeah," said Horace. "Not much out there even to cast a shadow."

Dunbar had not moved his fork. "Interesting all the same," he said.

"Horace has been here as long as anybody," I said. "He can tell you things other people can't."

Horace gave a small lift of the eyebrows. His blue-grey eyes were clear as he said, "Or won't."

Dunbar smiled again. "That's what I like, a man who isn't afraid to tell the truth. So tell me, where did the peaches come from?"

"From across the street. Dried."

"That's good. And before that?"

"For all I know, they could have come from Georgia or California or Arabia. It's beyond me."

"And me as well," said Dunbar. He took a bite of pie. "This is very good."

Horace said, "Thanks. Sometimes it seems as if you couldn't sell food in a famine in this town, but I'll tell you, whenever I bake a pie, it doesn't last more than a day. Word gets around."

Dunbar nodded. "Then it's a good thing we got here early in the day."

When we were out on the sidewalk again, Dunbar looked up and down the street. In an offhand tone he asked, "How does the marshal get along with Horace?"

"I don't think they cross paths much. The marshal takes his meals at the boarding house when he's in town. Why do you ask?"

"Just curious. You know how some lawmen are fond of sittin' around cafés and the like, and some proprietors are fond of givin' 'em free coffee."

"I don't think the marshal would be opposed to free coffee—or pie—but he and Horace aren't a natural pair. Neither are he and I, for that matter." After a few seconds' thought I added, "I wouldn't say that this town is divided. It's just that you don't have to be that close to get along."

"Just as well," said Dunbar. "And you never know what someone else might want."

We walked along the sidewalk in the shade. Out in the street the day was warming, but the air was cool, almost chilly, where we walked. I caught a trace of woodsmoke from somebody's cook stove. Maybe Horace was stoking his for the noon meal.

Dunbar and I walked past an empty building, and the blank windows gave me the illusion that our steps sounded more hollow. We passed the barbershop and I waved to Ted, who sat in his barber chair and rotated a few degrees as he waved back.

At the corner, Dunbar paused and stretched as he gave a casual glance up and down the street. "Quiet, all right," he said. Looking straight at me and not raising his voice, he asked, "What would be the best way of getting to talk to Doña Dolores?"

I lifted my hat and set it back about an inch, then twisted my mouth. "I happen to know the woman who works for her. We could go through her." I met his gaze. "I could ask."

"Thanks," he said. "I appreciate it."

"If you want, I can go there now, and we can meet back at my place."

"So much the better." He looked at the sun. "Time goes on. Even when you're not in a hurry."

"I'll see you in a little while, then." I turned and walked away.

I covered the few blocks to Doña Dolores's house in less than ten minutes. I stood in the shade and rapped on the door casing with my penknife, then settled back and lifted my hat to let the light perspiration cool.

The door opened, and Emilia appeared—always a pleasing sight to me. She was wearing the dark dress and white trim of a housemaid, one of the vestiges of Doña Dolores's earlier prosperity, and she had her hair tied back. But her facial features were bright and open, and her eyes sparkled as she spoke to me.

"Owen! What a surprise. Happy to see you."

"And happy to see you." I had the presence of mind to take off my hat.

"What can I help you with today?"

"It's for a friend. A visitor in town. He's staying at my place, and I think he has an interest in the quarry."

"Ohh."

"And he would like to visit with Doña Dolores, if she doesn't mind."

"I see." Emilia drew her brows together. "Would you like to ask her?"

I shrugged. "I don't know if it would be less trouble if I asked through you. That is, if you didn't mind."

"Not at all. I can ask." She held up her hand with her thumb and forefinger signifying a small amount. "Just a minute," she said. She closed the door behind her as she went into the house.

The door opened again after a couple of minutes. It looked as if Emilia had found time to dab her face and pat a few loose hairs into place. She held her head in a poised position as she smiled.

"Doña Dolores says she is willing to speak with your visitor."

Emilia spoke perfect English, but sometimes it seemed as if she spoke translated Spanish. Even at that, it was not out of place, as I knew that she and Doña Dolores spoke Spanish between them, and she had just come from speaking with the lady.

"Thank you," I said. "Is there a time that would be best?"

"Any time after the breakfast hour, or again after the dinner hour."

I knew that the dinner hour meant from one to three. "Would this afternoon be too soon?"

Emilia shook her head. "I don't think so."

"It might be convenient for my friend. His name, by the way, is Mr. Dunbar. Very much a gentleman." Now I felt as if I was speaking in translated Spanish, at least in tone.

"Very well. I'll let the *señora* know. You'll come with him?"

I winked. "Oh, yes. I wouldn't want him to get lost."

A smile played on her face. "Where does he come from?"

I imagined her picturing a Mr. Dunbar about five feet tall in a derby hat and polished shoes. "I don't know," I said. "I haven't asked. But he came here on horseback, and I don't think he gets lost very often."

"That's good." She moved back in the doorway and raised her hand. "I'll see you later, then."

"I'll look forward to it." I heard the door close as I went down the steps and put on my hat. I had a light, uplifted feeling as I walked back to the lodging house.

Dunbar was not there, but he came in a little later as I was slicing leftover cold beef for sandwiches. He took off his hat and sat down next to the table.

"There's plenty to see in this town, small though it is," he said.

"Oh, yes. Especially if you like looking in through the windows of empty buildings."

"The old Emporium across the street, for example."

"It was a good one. I remember when I was younger, say fifteen or sixteen, and I would see the ladies come and go. I would never have dreamed it would be empty like that, collecting dust."

"It's the last stone building as you go out of town to the west. All the others are on the two blocks in the center of town—on Main Street, at least."

I said, "That's correct. There are a few stone houses as well, of course."

"I saw a nice one. Set back from the street in the middle of the block. It must occupy two lots."

"Oh, yes. If you go from the Emporium toward the center of town, turn right at the corner, go all the way down the block to the livery stable, cross the street, turn left, and cross again, it's halfway down on your right."

Dunbar nodded. "That's the one."

"It was the Frenchman's house. We could call it his *maison. Maison de Pierre.*" I was proud of my own little joke.

"But his widow doesn't live there anymore, does she? You went somewhere else."

"No, Eliot, the banker, lives there, with his family. Doña Dolores lives a couple of blocks farther down. You'll see when we go there this afternoon."

"Oh. So you got us an appointment?"

"For you. I'll go along to show you the way, and then I'll cool my heels while you have your *tête-à-tête.*"

Dunbar gave me his shrewd look. "Something tells me that you won't suffer alone."

I shrugged. "Emilia and I have things to talk about, as we do some of the same kinds of work." I set the cutting board aside and turned to find my bread knife.

Dunbar waited as I sliced the bread and put together the first two sandwiches. When I was seated at the table, he spoke again.

"Maybe you could give me a little more background on the lady before I have my meeting with her. If you don't mind."

"Not at all. Some of this I've told you before, but here's a general sketch. Dolores comes from Santa Fe. An older family, I think. She looks more Spanish than Mexican, for those who care to know the difference. At any rate, she was educated, and she came here with the Carreau family. He came by way of Louisiana."

Dunbar nodded and said, "Mm-hmm" as he ate.

"I've told you how the wife died, and then the little boy, and then Carreau himself. He left Dolores the house and a small allowance. In order to make her means go farther, she sold the house and bought a more modest one, which you'll see later on."

Dunbar paused with his sandwich. "What did he do with the rest of his money?"

"Again, all I know is what I've heard. But he settled it in some complicated way on other members of his family. Sort of an old-country notion, I understood, that he didn't consider his money to be hers, and perhaps in part because she was not his first wife."

"Was there talk about her?"

"Oh, there was talk about her having *amours,* which I know nothing about, but she came here as a single woman, and she was very attractive. I remember that. And then there was another line of gossip. You know how people can be when they're envious." I paused to think of how to phrase it. "Because she knew French well enough to tutor the little boy, people whispered that she was Creole or Quadroon. As if there was anything wrong with that. But malice can make it seem that way. Still, she's Spanish. Just educated enough to know French."

"And paint and sing. And play the piano."

"Yes, although the joy went out of her life a long time ago."

"That's too bad," said Dunbar, "but I thank you for giving me this little bit of information. She probably doesn't own the quarry, then, does she?"

"Probably not. But it's a place to start."

"My thoughts, too. And I'm sure it'll be interesting to meet her."

Dunbar and I presented ourselves at Doña Dolores's door at a little past three that afternoon. Emilia let us in, and after we took off our hats, I introduced her and Dunbar to one another. She left us in the front room, in the company of two wooden armchairs with red velvet upholstery. I imagined them to have been carried over from the Carreau house.

Emilia excused herself and came back in a couple of minutes with the lady. I did not see Doña Dolores up close very often, but I was always struck by a sad expression she had, even when she was smiling, as she was now. It was a look I had seen on a couple of other women—one who had lost her two children in a fire, and one whose parents had died before her eyes at the hands of anarchists. Those women had adjusted, gone on through life, and smiled at the right moments. But there was something in the tenseness of the facial muscles, in the shadows around or behind their eyes, that seemed haunted.

So it was with Doña Dolores. Somewhere in her forties, she was still a handsome woman, with shoulder-length dark hair beginning to grey, dark eyes, a light tan complexion, and a figure that had not become matronly. Without looking quite straight at me, and maintaining her face in a half-smile, she held her hand forward and said, "Good afternoon. How nice of you to come."

"Good afternoon," I said, taking her hand and releasing it. "Thank you for agreeing to this visit. Please allow me to introduce Mr. Dunbar."

She gave him her hand and said, "Dolores Carreau."

He bowed halfway and straightened up. "J. R. Dunbar, and very pleased to meet you."

Silence hung for a few seconds until Dolores spoke. "Well, I understand you wished to visit with me about a matter."

"La Celeste," said Dunbar.

"Yes." She drew a breath. "I may not have a great deal to tell you, but if you'd like, we can speak in the next room."

"That would be fine."

"Very well." She turned to me. "Mr. Gregor, were you part of this conversation, or would you prefer to wait here?"

"I'll be happy to stay here," I said.

Dolores looked past me. "Emilia, you can attend to Mr. Gregor. If he would like something."

"Yes, lady."

I had a few seconds of entertainment as they spoke English to one another. I felt as if I was watching an amateur stage production and was seeing the actors rather than the characters. I always had a natural sympathy for Doña Dolores, and in this moment I felt that I knew her well enough to like her.

When the door closed, Emilia gestured at one of the red chairs. "Please sit down. Would you like something? A glass of water?"

"Nothing, thanks." I sat in the chair close by.

"Is it warm outside?"

"A little. Not bad."

"Did you come walking?"

"Yes. But it's not very far."

"That's good." After a pause she said, "You were right about your friend. He seems like a gentleman."

I felt a bit of pride in my association. "Oh, yes. He's very good."

"And do you have others staying there?"

"No, just him." I realized this was her way of asking after my family, so I said, "And Lalo? How is he?"

"Oh, he's fine. Just like always."

We sat for a minute or so without speaking, and I was trying to think of another topic when I heard voices rising in the next room. It sounded as if the conversation was coming to a close. Emilia and I looked at each other.

"That didn't take long," I said.

Emilia shrugged.

The door opened, and Dunbar walked through. He turned with his hat in his hands and said, "Thank you very much. I appreciate your help, and it's an honor to meet you." He gave his half-bow again.

Doña Dolores stood in the doorway. "And a pleasure for me. I'll do what I can."

I stood up, took leave of our hostess, and gave a lingering smile to Emilia as she held the door open for us.

Out on the street, I waited for Dunbar to speak. A breeze moved the air, and I noticed a yellow leaf here and there on the ground.

Half a block from the house, Dunbar said, "Very nice lady. Restrained, but very polite."

"Your conversation didn't last very long."

"It's like you said. Carreau left most of his property and assets entailed to other heirs. The quarry isn't hers, but she was gracious enough to offer to help me inquire further. She took my name and will pass it on. Not exactly a dead end, but it doesn't get me very far at the present."

"That's too bad."

"Oh, it's not that much trouble. I'm not in a hurry, and I've got other things to look into."

"Anything else for this afternoon?"

He took in a deep breath and gazed ahead in the distance. "Not that I can think of. Why?"

"Well, sometimes on a day like this, more often on a Saturday, I fetch a bottle of beer from the saloon and sit in the shade of my back yard. But I wouldn't want to corrupt you."

"It would take more than that," he said.

"That's why I don't propose that we sit in the saloon."

The sun had gone far enough south in its yearly course that the back yard of the lodging house lay in shadow even in midafternoon. Dunbar sat in an old wooden chair with his hat cocked at a jack-deuce angle and his boot hiked onto his knee. I sat in a similar posture with my hat resting on my upraised knee. Pedro wandered at the end of his tether and nibbled weeds.

A low, wailing sound came from the alleyway to our right. Dunbar brushed away a fly and glanced at me. The sound came again. Dunbar made a small frown and gave me a questioning look. The sound came again, a floating *Ah-woo-woo.*

"That's Lalo," I said.

"Lalo?"

"Short for Leonardo. Emilia's brother."

"Oh." Dunbar settled back in his chair.

The sound died away, and a couple of minutes later I heard a footstep on dry ground. I pretended not to look, but I could see a form behind the clump of hollyhocks at the corner of the neighbor's property.

The sound carried again, softer now, softer than a dove's call. *Ah-woo-oo.*

When it ended, I called out in Spanish. "Is that you, Lalo?"

Ah-woo-oo.

"Is that a mouse, or is that you, Lalo?"

I heard motion behind the hollyhocks, then a laugh. A slender human form stepped into view. Lalo had short, dark hair, no hat, a short-sleeved shirt, baggy pants, and sandals. He laughed again, almost a boy's giggle.

I set my beer bottle aside and stood up. Still in Spanish, I said, "Lalo, what are you doing? Did you come to see me? What do you have?"

He brought his hand out from behind him and showed two rigid corn tortillas.

"Oh, Pedro likes you," I said.

Lalo smiled and went through the open gate and into the shed. He came out with Pedro's battered tin feed dish and put the two tortillas in it. As he walked toward Pedro, the donkey lifted his head, turned, and stuck his nose in the dish. Crunching sounds followed, then the gentler, nicking sounds as Pedro cleaned up the crumbs.

Lalo put his arm around Pedro's neck and said, "You can give him to me."

"Why would I do that?" I asked.

"Maybe you don't want him anymore."

"And why would I not want him?"

Lalo glanced at Dunbar and back at me. "You ride the fine horse. You don't need a burro anymore. You can give him to me."

"Of course I need my burro. The horse belongs to this gentleman. And I love Pedro. I know you love him, but I do, too. You know that." I cast an eye at Dunbar, and I could tell he understood this was a thirty-year-old man with the mind of a child. "Look, Lalo," I went on. "You could have your own burro. You need to save your money. You work. You pick up stones, you clean stables, you dig holes and trenches. But you spend all your money on candy. Tell your sister not to let you do that. Do you want me to tell her? Then she won't let you give all your money to Horace."

Lalo hung his head and smiled in his boyish way. He patted Pedro's neck. "You ride the fine horse."

"It is this man's horse."

Dunbar rose from his chair. I thought Lalo might say something to him in English. When he was not working, which was most of the time, Lalo wandered around. He did not go into other people's yards or houses, but he saw and heard a great many things, which he then reported to Horace, or the blacksmith, or the stable man, or anyone else who would listen to his halting English.

Dunbar spoke first, and in Spanish. "Look," he said. "This is what he likes." He reached forward and rubbed Pedro on the ridge of his forehead between his ears, then down on the broad area between his eyes. "Do him like this, like his mother did. See? He likes it."

Dunbar stepped back, and Lalo rubbed the donkey's forehead.

Lalo said, "It's true that he likes it."

"You're his friend," said Dunbar.

"That's true."

"We're all friends," I said.

CHAPTER THREE

A kerosene lamp added brightness to the morning light at breakfast. Dunbar was making neat work of getting rhubarb jam out of the crockery jar when he said, "What do you know about the Harvey ranch?"

I took a drink of coffee. "It's about ten miles west of here. South of the Rock Canyon Ranch and farther out. It's a hardscrabble place, but Old Man Harvey has had it for a long time, so I guess it supports something."

"What would you think of taking a ride out there? I'd like to ask about antelope hunting."

I wondered about a ten-mile ride. My legs had been sore for a day after the short trip out to the Frenchman's Quarry. I said, "I suppose I could. It's been a long time since I've shot an antelope, but I'd be happy to serve as your *aide-de-camp.*"

"Oh, I wouldn't plan on shooting anything today. Just ask about it and look around a little."

"Maybe it'll let me get my riding legs back. I hadn't ridden for quite a while when we went out the other day."

"We'll take it easy. No hard ridin' unless we decide to rope a coyote."

We finished breakfast, and I cleaned up the kitchen as Dunbar got ready for the day. He was like a man who had a ledger to write in, though I doubted that he would write down anything that someone else could see. He kept to himself for periods of time, as if he sorted information in the way that another person would sort buttons, and it seemed to me that he kept a full inventory under his hat.

The morning air was cool when we walked outside. We crossed the street in the middle of the block, went past the blank windows of the Emporium, and turned at the corner. We continued down the block to the livery stable, where a man was leaning against a post that held up the overhang. He was on the other side of the post, so I couldn't see for sure who he was.

As we walked past him, I confirmed what I had thought. The man was Lee Porter, the hired man at Pat Roderick's ranch. I didn't care to try to make conversation, so I just said, "Mornin' " as we walked past.

"Goin' out?" he asked.

Now we had to stop.

Porter stayed leaning against the post. He was a man of about forty, average height and build, with light brown hair and mustache and light brown eyes. He wore a dust-colored hat, a light brown wool vest, and a faded wheat-colored canvas jacket. He raised a cigarette to his lips as he looked at us.

"My friend Dunbar would like to go out and see a little of the country," I said.

Porter squinted against the cigarette smoke as he took a drag. He blew the smoke away and nodded. "Lots of it out there," he said. He made a small, wrinkling motion with his nose as he looked at Dunbar. "I'm the foreman at the Rock Canyon Ranch."

"How do you do," said Dunbar.

"If you get over that way, I can show you around."

Dunbar made busy work of snugging his gloves. He raised his eyes and said, "That would be a pleasure."

Porter looked at me. "Which way are you going?"

"Out by Harvey's," I said.

"Have a good ride." Porter lowered his hand so that his

thumb rested on his holster. A thin curl of smoke rose from his cigarette.

"Thanks," I said, and we went into the stable.

The sun was warming the day, though not very fast, as we rode out of town.

"What's the foreman's name?" Dunbar asked.

"Lee Porter. And I don't know what kind of a foreman he is. As far as I know, he's the only one who works there."

Dunbar pursed his lips so that his mustache went up. He said, "I've been on a couple of ranches, and it seems to me that a foreman gets his status or authority by the number of men he has beneath him. Like a pyramid."

"Then he's like the tip of a pyramid with no base. I wonder about him offering to show us around."

Dunbar shrugged and gave a light smile. "You never know when we might take him up on it."

We reached the Harvey ranch in the latter part of the morning. I had already told Dunbar not to expect to meet the old man, as he was not very sociable. As we rode into the ranch yard, the sound of someone beating on metal came from inside the barn. A dog came out and barked at us, and the banging stopped. A man in a wide-brimmed hat appeared at the barn door. He stood straight up and held a hand sledge at his side, and though he was smudged from his work, he was way too clean to be Old Man Harvey.

The man called at the dog and waved us in. I raised my hand in greeting and said to Dunbar, "That's the hired man."

We rode a little farther, then dismounted and walked in. A horse whinnied from inside the barn.

"Hello, Jum," I said. "What are you up to?"

"Tryin' to shoe a horse. And you?" He tipped his head up. He had a prominent nose, wide ears, a loose bandana, and an unbuttoned vest. His work shirt was half-tucked in, and he was not wearing a gun.

"Just came out to see the country," I said. "My friend Mr. Dunbar has an interest in the antelope population."

"Thinnin' it out, I hope." He shifted the hammer to his other hand and reached out to shake. "Jum Bailey," he said.

"J. R. Dunbar. Pleased to meet you."

Jum moved his head up and down, and a short toothpick showed in the corner of his mouth. "You can get 'em just about any time. Mornin's good. Seems like they lay up in the middle part of the day, and then you see 'em about three, four in the afternoon." He gave a toss of the head. "Just have at it. Don't shoot no cows, of course."

"Oh, we won't," I said. "We weren't planning to hunt today anyway. Just look around."

Dunbar spoke up. "What do I need to know about boundaries?"

"Not much. The old man's got three sections. Beyond that, it's open range, but it all looks the same. And the antelope sure don't know any difference. You get too close to Roderick's place, you might want to check with him. His range doesn't cover all that much, but he gets a little jealous."

"We've met Lee," I said.

"Then it won't be hard to ask. Or maybe you already did."

"Not yet."

The horse in the barn whinnied again, and Jum said, "Well, that's about it." He looked at both of us. "Anything else?"

"Not today," said Dunbar. "Is there anything we can give you a hand with while we're out here?"

"I don't know what it would be."

Dunbar flicked the ends of his reins. "We might move along, then. Let you do your work."

"Oh, no hurry. But I 'magine you've got things to see. Come back any time."

"Thanks." Dunbar turned to me. "Ready?"

"Yep." I led the buckskin horse out a few steps, lifted my foot into the stirrup, and heaved myself up onto the saddle.

When Dunbar saw that I was aboard, he pulled himself into the saddle with one hand and swung his horse around. We waved to Jum Bailey and rode out of the yard.

Partway back to town, Dunbar suggested that we ride by a windmill that was visible in the southeast. When we rode to it and dismounted, he loosened the cinch on the blue roan, and I did the same on the buckskin.

A breeze was stirring, so the blades on the windmill made a slow whirring sound, and the rod creaked as it went up and down. Water spilled out of the pipe in a trickle.

After the horses drank, Dunbar took off his hat and gloves. He bent to the tank and splashed water on his face, then wiped off his mustache and stood up.

"Feels good," he said. "Water's cool. Go ahead." He stood back with his head up and his palms open, in an attitude of drying off.

In that moment I noticed something that I had seen before but hadn't thought about. In the palm of his right hand, Dunbar had a dark spot, as if he had been branded or burned in the hand at some time in the past. I must have noticed it now because his hand was damp and the spot was darker. He did not seem to make any attempt to either show it or not let it be seen, so I paid it no more attention. I set my hat on my saddle horn and washed my face.

The sun was straight up, so I took out some biscuits and cheese I had brought along. The windmill hummed and creaked in its lonesome way as we sat on the ground holding our reins and eating our lunch.

After taking a long look out across the plain, Dunbar said, "There's one thing I still don't have a good count on."

"What's that?"

"Nothing personal, but the other day you said there were three people in town who spoke Spanish. Now that I've met them, I assume you meant Dolores, Emilia, and Lalo."

"That's right."

"Yet I'm sure I heard you speaking Spanish yesterday to Lalo."

"I guess I did."

"I just wondered."

"It never occurred to me to include myself. If I were to adjust that figure now, I would have to say five, because I'm sure I heard you doing the same."

"Better to leave it as it is, then. I don't count for much, and one of these days I'll be gone." He took a bite of biscuit and cheese.

"Do you think you'll shoot an antelope before you go?"

"Hah. I don't know what I'd do with all the meat. But it's an idea. Like a lot of other things." An amused expression came onto his face. "I've heard of sport hunters donating the meat to a jail, but I don't suppose Mr. Roderick keeps a very full house."

"Hardly ever has anyone in there."

"Yet he keeps his job."

I said, "There are a few businesses that have a little more interest to protect. The bank and the general store, to begin with. Then there's the saloon, and after that the boarding house and the café. I'm at the lowest level, and I pay just a pittance, but everybody pays something. Residents, too. I think Emilia pays a dollar a year. The fees cover the jail as well as the general presence of the law."

"So if marauders ever came to town, everything would be protected. Beginning with the bank."

"That's the idea. But there are smaller things as well. Make sure people don't leave dead animals lying around or peek into one another's windows. He has to tend to all of that."

"No mayor?"

"No. The main businessmen get together when they need to—by the way, Ted the barber is part of the group."

"I see."

"So we have kind of a town council, and the rest of us go along. There's really not much to argue about."

"So that's what you meant when you said the town wasn't divided."

"Right. There's this group that hangs together a little tighter, but there's only so much they could do, even if they wanted to have an iron rule. The others wouldn't put up with it."

Dunbar nodded. "I can imagine people taking their money out of the bank and traveling forty miles to buy their broomsticks and bacon. I've heard of people doing that."

"So have I. It's petty, but sometimes things come to that."

We finished our meal and went on our way. Haze began to gather in the sky above, and the sun lost some of its brightness. The air was still warm, though, and no clouds were forming in the west or the north where the storms came from at this time of the year. As we rode on, the air felt a little heavier, and the afternoon became one of those drowsy times when even the grasshoppers seemed to move in slow motion as they spread their pale wings and clicked away. The footfalls of the horses sounded dull on the dry earth, and the odor of sagebrush hung on the air.

A jackrabbit got up from behind a clump of soapweed, and my horse spooked. It jerked to one side and bolted, plunging for a half-dozen strides as I hung onto my saddle horn and fumbled to keep hold of my reins. I got the horse stopped at about the time it would have slowed down anyway.

I rode back to the spot where Dunbar waited.

"Everything all right?" he asked.

"Oh, yeah."

"You didn't even lose your hat. That's good." His dark eyes were looking me over, and I had the feeling that he saw me as a stranger on his horse.

His eyes relaxed, and he let go of his reins with his left hand and flexed it. He was wearing his yellowish leather gloves as usual, and the action put me in mind of the dark spot I had seen in the palm of his hand—his other hand, now that I thought of it.

As we rode onward, I wondered how such a mark came to be. I had read of people being branded in the hand—transported felons in colonial times, Negro slaves in the South before the war. I tried to imagine Dunbar laboring to build one of the great Pyramids, being chained as a galley slave in Roman times, or even being hauled up in front of a secret society that met by torchlight, but none of it fit. Neither did the idea of his being a wild-eyed photographer or chemist holding a puddle of caustic liquid in his hand. I set those fancies aside and observed him as he rode his blue horse and looked out across the grassland. Still, I could not see him as just an ordinary cowpuncher who had happened to be burned in the hand.

My thoughts returned to normal when we came to the old railroad bed and I realized the Frenchman's Quarry was only a mile or so to our right.

"Say," I called across to Dunbar. "What would you think of going past the quarry?"

"The Celeste? Why not? If you've got the time, I sure do. Are you not getting tired?"

"It's not very far out of the way. I thought you might like to have another look at it, and I wouldn't mind seeing that picture of the stonecutter again."

We turned our horses and rode to the southeast. Half a mile later, the tops of the two old buildings came into view. We rode to the right where the ground rose, and in a few more minutes the quarry was visible. The broad, shallow pit stretched more than a quarter-mile across to the buildings. We kept to the higher ground and went around on the south edge, then came at the buildings from the east side.

We tied the horses at the rail and went into the office area. I kept my head up, with the idea of not breathing in so much dust. I saw the lithograph of the stonecutter right away and was about to go around the counter when Dunbar's voice came out in a sharp tone.

"Whoa! What's this?"

I stopped short and looked down. On the floor in front of us, a pair of feet, or rather black shoes, pointed up.

"Don't touch anything," said Dunbar.

"I won't." I stood there as he did, studying.

The body was that of a younger man, maybe twenty-five years old. He was dressed better than a working-class man, as he wore a lightweight, light-blue jacket that matched his creased pants. He wore a white shirt, open at the neck, and had dark hair. A shadow on his pale face showed where he had shaved on the last day of his life, and his eyelids were closed. He was lying on his back with his arms at his sides, and he had a soft look about him as if he had not been troubled much by physical labor.

"He looks pretty clean," said Dunbar. "No signs of stabbing or shooting or beating, unless there's something on the back of his head, and I'm not going to move him." Dunbar's dark eyes moved around the room. "Not much dust has been disturbed, either. My guess is that someone left him here. It's a cinch he didn't walk here himself, lie down to take a rest, and expire. He's got no hat, and he doesn't have the kind of dust that a traveler would. Not even on his shoes." Dunbar knelt. He pushed with a gloved finger against the side of the sole of a polished shoe. "A little stiff. He's probably been here all day, but not much longer." Dunbar stood up. "What's he look like to you?"

I let out a breath, as if I had been holding it for a long time. "A dead man," I said. I raised my eyes and saw the stonecutter in the picture, with his pointed beard and his pointed hammer. I had the impression he was working on someone's gravestone. I looked again at the dead man with his dark hair, shadowy pale face, and faded red lips. The rest of the world seemed to be far away. "Actually," I said, "he looks like a Frenchman."

"That's what I thought."

I glanced around the dusty room with the same cobwebs I had seen a couple of days earlier. I said, "Other than that, he's way out of place. Makes me wonder if someone left him here with the idea of stashing him or of making him easy to find."

Dunbar had his eyebrows raised. "There's better places to hide a body if that was what someone wanted to do."

Back in town, we found Marshal Roderick standing with his hands on his hips as he watched two men rolling a barrel of coal oil from a freight wagon onto the platform behind the mercantile store. The merc, as people called it, was once a separate business but was now combined with the general store under a single ownership. It still had inventory from the quarry days, such as a two-man crowbar that was now a curiosity, but it also had everyday merchandise such as coal oil, fence wire, and chains. Ross Ferguson, the general store owner, was standing next to Roderick and watching the work with heavy-lidded eyes. The marshal did not seem inclined to detach himself from Ferguson, so the store owner heard the report as I gave it.

Ferguson's eyes opened as he gazed at the marshal. Roderick kept his eyes on me, ignoring Dunbar, as he said, "I can understand why you're telling me this, but it's outside my jurisdiction."

"The death itself might well have happened in town here," I said.

The marshal took a full breath and drew himself up, as he liked to do, to look down at me. "If it happened in my town, and I knew about it, I'd do something about it. Believe me."

Dunbar spoke. "Chances are that he was in this town. Someone might have seen him. He might even have stayed over. He's got to have a valise or something somewhere. It wouldn't hurt to ask around."

Ferguson's eyes narrowed. "It wouldn't be too much. See if anyone knows anything. We can send Ted out there to pick up the body. I don't see anything wrong with paying him his fee, even if it is out of town. Someone's got to do something. You don't just leave a man to rot."

The marshal shook his head with authority. "Of course not. I just don't like—"

Ferguson turned to the working men and barked, "Careful there!" Back to Roderick, he said, "I'll let Ted know. You can ask around." He turned back to us. "That's good enough for right now. We'll find out about it."

Dunbar and I walked the horses to the livery stable and put them away. Back at the lodging house, he stretched and yawned.

"I think I'm goin' to rest for a while," he said.

"Me, too. That took a little out of me."

Dunbar went to his room, and I stretched out on the old divan in the sitting room. Within a few minutes I was asleep.

When I awoke, the room was dimmer than before. I checked my watch and saw that I had slept for more than an hour. I got up, startled. It was time to get things going for the evening meal, and I needed some groceries. I rapped on Dunbar's door to let him know I was going out, but he didn't answer. I put on my hat and went on my errand.

The shadows of late afternoon had stretched to the middle of the street, and no one was stirring. A single horse stood hipshot in front of the saloon. I did not meet anyone as I walked the two blocks to the general store.

Ben, the clerk, took my order and went about gathering the items. As I waited, Ross Ferguson came in from the mercantile side and sat at his desk beyond the counter. He paid me no attention but rather busied himself with a stack of papers.

I walked over and said, "Any news?"

He made a slow turn of the head and looked at me through his half-closed eyes. "News?"

"Of the dead man."

"Oh, that. Well, Ted's gone out to get him."

"Anything here in town?"

Ferguson seemed to consider whether he had to tell me anything. Then he said, "Turns out he was here, or someone like him. Spent the night in the boarding house. They didn't see him this morning, but his bag was still there."

"Then they must have found a name for him."

Ferguson stared at his papers, drummed his fingers once, and said, "He registered as Philip Gaston. Some papers among his things have the same name, with an address of Baton Rouge, Louisiana."

"Oh."

"That's all I know."

"Well, thanks."

"Don't mention it." He went back to his papers.

Ben had set the bread and canned tomatoes on the counter and was wrapping the ham. He spoke as he worked. "Too bad about the young fella, huh? Come from Louisiana to die in a place like this. That's where the old Frenchman was from. Wonder if they're related. Marshal sent a wire. You know, you can ship the body, and the family can pay the freight on their end. No reason we should have to. Wonder what he was doing

49

here. Maybe it was his quarry. You know, the widow doesn't own it."

"Any idea how he died?"

"If it's his quarry, maybe he walked out there to take a look at it and got bit by a rattlesnake. Those rocky places are good for that. Easier to get bit by a snake than to get shot in this town. I don't believe there's been a shooting in all the time I've lived here."

I said, "The little French boy drowned, didn't he?"

Ross Ferguson turned in his chair and gave me a cross look with his heavy eyes.

Ben said, "I don't know. That was before I came here."

When I was out on the sidewalk and headed back, I saw the marshal come out of the jail. It was a small stone building across the street and down on the corner. I figured he had been watching. He crossed over and met me when I reached the corner on my side.

"Hello, Pat," I said.

"Afternoon."

"I guess we got some information on young Mr. Gaston," I said.

"News travels fast."

"Hard to sit on it in this town."

The marshal's face went hard. "I'd like to know if you and your friend had anything to do with this."

"Oh, go on," I said. "The body had been there for hours when we found it."

"He disappeared sometime between midnight and sunup."

"I don't know anything about that. We both slept at the lodging house, and I fixed breakfast. Your own hired man can tell you what time we rode out of town, and Jum Bailey can tell you what time we were at the Harvey ranch."

"I don't need to ask Jum Bailey a damn thing." The marshal

moved close and looked down into my face. He was seething as he said, "If I find out this man died in town, and if it turns out you had a hand in it, you'll be back in prison for the rest of your life."

I could feel my hands shaking, but I pulled myself together. I said, "I don't know where you'll get your proof, because there isn't any. Unless someone makes it up."

Roderick's eyes bored right into me, and his words were slow as he said, "I'd like to knock your teeth down your throat."

"Careful there!" It was Dunbar's voice, calm and controlled.

The marshal's voice changed, and I thought I heard a quaver as he said, "You stay out of this."

"I'm in it, at least as long as you're leaning on my friend here."

Roderick's jaw muscles tensed. His voice was steadier as he said, "I don't need you or anyone else to tell me how to do my job."

"I'm sure you don't, and maybe you've already heard what I have."

"What was that?"

Dunbar shrugged. "I was in the Desert Rose Café, and Horace just happened to mention that he was in the Diamond Saloon last night. He calls it the tavern, but it's the only drinking establishment in town."

"Well, what of it?"

"He says the young Frenchman was in there, asking questions about one thing and another."

The marshal's face was hard as granite. He said, "You know, we didn't have any trouble until you came to town. I wouldn't be surprised if either or both of you had something to do with this."

Dunbar said, "Oh, don't try that. You'd be better off saying you didn't have any trouble until Philip Gaston came to town,

51

asking questions. He wanted to know who owned the quarry and who owned the big house that Pierre Carreau used to live in." Dunbar paused. "And he asked about how the little Carreau boy died. He drowned, didn't he?"

Roderick's teeth were clenched, and he released them. "Yes, he did. It was a long time ago. And the man who was responsible went to prison."

CHAPTER FOUR

I had my back to the table and was slicing ham, cutting through the rind and carving around the bone, when Dunbar caught me off guard with a question.

"So who was the man who went to prison? For the death of the little Carreau boy."

I got my composure back. I turned, and with the knife in my hand I said, "His name was Tim Sexton. As I mentioned before, I was away at the time. In fact, I was in prison myself, but it wasn't for anything I did here. I'll tell you about it some other time." I thought he might have heard the marshal's comment, so I added, "It's no secret. And Roderick loves having it over me."

"I can imagine."

I waved the knife. "Anyway, back to the story. This fellow Tim Sexton worked in the Emporium across the way. He was very fond of Dolores when she was still single, and I think she returned some of his attention. But she married Carreau, and as you can imagine, Tim was very dejected about it." I put a frying pan on the stove to heat the slices of ham. Dunbar nodded for me to go on.

"Then the little boy died. It was terrible. Even when I heard about it, much later, I was haunted by the idea of him and his blond, wavy hair floating in the horse trough. Some people thought it was an accident, and some people thought it was caused. The boy's father almost went crazy. He blamed Dolores, and he blamed Tim. He accused him more than once. There was a big investigation, and finally they found someone who said he saw Tim pushing the boy in the direction of the horse trough."

"And who was the witness?"

"No one I knew, though I heard his name later. Dade Flynn. Someone who lived here at the time and moved on."

"So they found Tim guilty and sent him off to prison."

"That's right. It satisfied some people but not others. Not long afterwards, the quarry went out of production, and then Carreau died. Quite despondent, I'm sure. Dolores has lived under a cloud ever since."

"And this all took place about twenty years ago?"

"Yes. The boy died just a little over twenty years ago."

"Then Philip Gaston would have been close in age to the little Carreau boy."

"Oh, yes. What a thing to think about. Little André would be about that age if he had lived. And yet it all figures up. He and Lalo played together, though Lalo was a few years older."

"Did Emilia work for the first Mrs. Carreau?"

"I don't think so. I believe she went to work for Doña Dolores after the Frenchman died. But at some point, Lalo knew André."

"But he didn't see him die, though."

"Oh, no. I'm sure of that. If he did, we would have heard the story a thousand times."

Dunbar was out and about for most of the next day. He left right after breakfast, and he came back at dusk. From his appearance I guessed he had been to the barbershop for a shave, but I didn't think it had taken him all day.

"What news?" I asked.

"Well, they got the body shipped. I'm sure nobody wanted to

waste time. Ted the barber collected his fee for bringing the body to town and then for taking it to the train stop, so he's happy. The marshal and Mr. Ferguson and Mr. Eliot the banker got rid of the body before it began to putrefy, so they're happy."

"It must have been a long shave."

"Ted's the type that turns you around to face the mirror and talks to you that way."

"I know. He does that with me when he cuts my hair."

"But he does like to talk, so that's good. Even if he slants things in favor of your informal town council, he values the coin of the common man. I tipped him, of course."

I laughed. "That's all for the best. While you were at it, did he happen to mention the cause of death?"

"He did. As you probably know, he signs a certificate. Actually two in cases like this one. The marshal keeps a copy and sends one with the body."

"And his opinion was—?"

"Unknown causes. No signs of violence, none of the more obvious signs of poisoning. Vomit, drool—you know."

"Uh-huh. So what's your guess?"

"Smothering, or etherization of some kind, like chloroform. Just a guess, though."

"Did the lather get dry?"

Dunbar frowned. "How do you mean?"

"You were gone all day. I can't help being curious."

"Oh. I took a ride down the line about twenty miles to that little stop called Milton." He paused, and when I didn't say anything, he went on. "I was able to send a telegram and get an answer without having the news beat me back to the saloon."

"I see."

"I was able to find out that Philip Gaston is indeed from Baton Rouge, Louisiana. He does not have any known relation to Mr. Carreau, who came here by way of Lafayette, though I would guess there is some connection. At any rate, he is not among the heirs in Pierre Carreau's will."

I gave Dunbar a close look. "Are you some kind of a Pinkerton man?"

"No, I work on my own." He smiled. "As you well know, I'm a sporting man. What do you think of taking a ride out to look at some deer country tomorrow? Are your legs getting better?"

"I think they'll be all right tomorrow."

We were out on the range by shortly after breakfast the next morning. Dunbar seemed to know where he was going, or at least in what general direction. He steered a course west toward the foothills, keeping to the south of the Rock Canyon Ranch and to the north of Harvey's ranch. Twice we saw antelope at a distance of a couple of hundred yards. The first time, a doe and a fawn trotted away. The second time, a group of three, led by a buck, turned and ran to the south, their light colors flashing in the morning sun.

We stopped at midmorning to let the horses drink at a windmill. The country was enjoying a stretch of sunny days after the first squall of chilly, damp weather. We hadn't had a first frost yet, but the mornings started out cool. By this time of day, the grasshoppers had their blood flowing, and the flies and gnats were humming around the water tank.

"Nice country," I said, looking back over the rangeland in the direction of town. "So calm and peaceful. You wonder about people who always have things in turmoil."

Dunbar rubbed his gloved hand against his cheekbone. "They take it with 'em wherever they go. You'd think living in the country was simple and city life was complicated, or the mountains were a place a man could go to when things on the plains got to grinding away on him. But the truth is, life is what people make of it wherever they go. It would be bad enough if they just made it for themselves, like the fella who sits in a dark house all day and feels sorry for himself. But some people have got to reach out and tangle up others. That's the difference. Nature minds its own business. People don't."

I said, "Just for the sake of argument, we want to remember those who reach out and do good to one another. Not that I've lived much among 'em, you understand."

"Neither have I. And I've had occasion to meet a few of them that aren't all what they seem. But I'll grant you those that do good. For the sake of argument."

We rode on through the rest of the morning and found a bluff that gave shade at midday. Not far to the west, the foothills rose with trees scattered along the flanks.

"This is more likely deer country," I said.

"Yes, it is. I've been through some of the country west of here, awhile back. You go another forty miles, which we won't do today, and you get into big country—canyons, rocks, streams. I know of a place up there, a solid log ranch house with barns and corrals and a creek flowing down through a meadow. Like I was saying earlier. A fella went up there, took all of his bile and poison with him, and ruined half a dozen lives before he went down. It'll take a generation or more for the memories to die out of that place."

"I'm not familiar with the ranches out this way," I said. "Was there a place you knew of where you wanted to stop today?"

"Oh. Sorry for all the cheerful talk. No, I didn't have a place in mind. I just hadn't been over on this side, and I wanted to see what it was like between here and town. And look for deer, of course."

We ate the cold biscuits and dried apples I had brought along. Dunbar said he would like to take a look around, so I sat in the shade and looked after the horses as he climbed up on a rocky outcropping. He took out a small pair of binoculars and studied the country in all directions. After about fifteen minutes he came down, and we headed back.

With Dunbar taking the lead, we angled north for about a mile and then rode almost straight east where the country made a gradual slope downward toward town. The horses moved at a brisk walk, and each time I turned to look back, the foothills were farther away.

At a little past midafternoon, Dunbar drew his horse to a stop and said, "It looks like we're gettin' close to where the marshal's quarry ought to be. What would you think of droppin' by for a look at it?"

"Do you think we'd be needling him?"

"Not that he could say. After all, his foreman did give us an open invitation."

"I guess he did."

"Have you been out here before?" he asked.

"Only once that I can remember, and that was before the marshal bought it. As I recall, coming from town, you get to the ranch house first. Then farther up the canyon is the quarry. They say the house he's building is between the two."

"Let's give it a look."

I followed him over a couple of low, bare hills where small bits of rock lay all about and the blades of grass were a hand's width apart. Ahead of us, a canyon opened up out of a hillside, and I saw the first of the stone walls of Bluestone Quarry. We followed a cow trail downhill and turned back west when we came to the floor of the canyon.

The quarry was not a neat, hollow excavation like the Frenchman's was. It had a floor, but there were piles of rock and standing formations everywhere, with paths leading among them like narrow streets in a city of stones. I searched my memory for the word, and it came up. *Necropolis*. City of the dead.

Dunbar swung down from his horse, and I did the same.

"Quite a place," I said in a low voice.

"There's a lot of rock." Dunbar's spurs jingled and his boot soles crunched as he walked forward.

I followed, and as the pathway widened I came alongside him. The sandstone glared in the sun and had a darker yellow hue in the shadows. We stopped for a moment, and just as we were moving forward again, a man stepped from behind a column of rock.

It was Lee Porter, the hired man, not quite blocking the way as he stood with his thumb on his gunbelt. Smoke curled up from a cigarette he held there.

"What do you need?" he asked.

Dunbar said, "After your invitation the other day, we thought we'd take you up on it and drop in."

"No harm in that." Porter was dusty as usual and had about two days' worth of light-colored stubble where the grey was beginning to show. He turned to me. "Hard ride?"

"Not so much."

"You've got to be careful comin' in here on your own," he said to us both. "Farther back, there's a pit. It's got slickrock sides, like a mine shaft, only wider, and a dark pool at the bottom. Back when they first started takin' rock out of here, with mules, they lost a couple down in there. Might have swallowed a Chinaman or two as well."

"Right down the gullet," said Dunbar.

"I'd show it to you, but it's pretty snaky back in there at this time of the year. Come back in a month or so, when the snakes are denned up, and we can take a look. Maybe even find a snake that's sleepin', or a ball of 'em, and throw 'em in there. I do that sometimes."

Dunbar said, "I don't care much for snakes. We were out lookin' at deer country. I prefer to hunt them a little later, too, when the snakes have gone in."

Porter sniffed. "Me, I've got to put up with 'em. I can't pick when I work."

"Is your boss at home?"

"Um, no. He's at work in town. Why?"

Dunbar shrugged. "Oh, we thought we'd ride out by way of the house."

"Well, he's not there. I'll ride that way with you, though." Porter walked past the column he had come out from behind and continued past a square base of rock the size of a homesteader's shack. He went behind the formation and came out with a sorrel ranch horse. After tossing a look at us, he flipped the reins in place and swung aboard. As he rode past us, he said, "This way."

The canyon narrowed to a mouth and opened up on a flat where the stone house was in progress. It reminded me of the *maison* in the picture except that it had unfinished doorways and windows that looked like decapitated columns. As it had been in progress for a few years, it did not have a new look about it. Weeds grew on the floor, and piles of rubble lay among the larger stone. All in all, it looked more like a structure falling down than one going up, something like illustrations I had seen of old castles and abbeys.

In a moment we were past it, and when I looked back, it seemed to be standing at the gateway to the city of stones.

A couple of hundred yards further brought us to the ranch yard, where the wooden house stood unimpressive. Porter stopped his horse and said, "It's good of you to drop by. Come again. I'm almost always around somewhere."

"You bet," said Dunbar.

"Thanks," I said. This time I rode on without looking back.

★　★　★　★　★

Dunbar and I put away a good portion of ham and boiled potatoes after our day's ride. When supper was finished, he sat musing as I washed the dishes and cleaned up the kitchen. He had his hands together in front of him on the table, upright with the tips of his index fingers touching. It reminded me of the children's game of "This is the church, and this is the steeple." When I sat down, he laid his hands flat on the table as if he was waiting for cards.

"Here's an idea," he said. "It's Saturday. Might be a good time to drop in on the tavern, as Horace calls it."

"The Diamond Saloon," I offered.

"I got a look at it the other day when we stopped in for the beer, but those places are different at night."

"Yes," I said. "For one thing, he'll have a couple of more lanterns lit."

Dunbar's hands moved, but he did not drum his fingers or fidget. "I think I might go. How about you?"

"I could go along. I don't like to spend all night in those places."

"Neither do I."

The interior of the Diamond Saloon was lit up with a row of four lanterns hanging from the rafters above the bar. The light carried out to the middle of the floor, and things got dimmer at the edges and in the corners. The bar sat against the back wall, where a set of heavy shelves rose up on either side of a mirror three feet wide and five feet tall. The man behind the bar was Jim Sloane, the proprietor. He wiped the bar in front of us and said, "Gentlemen. What'll it be?"

I said, "A glass of whiskey for me."

"Same for me," said Dunbar. He laid a silver dollar on the counter, and looking at me, he said, "You paid last time."

I laughed. "That was part of the lodging. I put it on your bill."

"No harm in that."

I thought Dunbar might be repeating Lee Porter's words, but he gave no expression that would let me know. When Sloane had the drinks poured, I said, "We'll take these to a table."

Sloane did not look at me as he said, "You should have told me." He rang the cash box.

"Keep the change," said Dunbar.

We walked to a table off to one side, not in direct light and not next to the pathway between the front door and the bar. Half a dozen other patrons were in the place, four at a table and two with a foot on the rail. I had a passing recognition of all six, having seen them at one time or another when they came in from the ranches.

Dunbar assumed an air of idleness, and when the four men at the table began to sing a version of "The Red-Eye Saloon," he swayed his head and tapped his foot. The words floated through the haze of tobacco smoke.

> *I landed in Rawlins with nothin' to do,*
> *So I took a walk down to the Red-Eye Saloon.*

Dunbar tossed me a casual glance and said, "Who's the chap in the corner?"

I frowned as a way of saying I didn't know. I gave a slow turn and peered into the corner on the far side of the door. In the shadows I made out a figure I had not seen earlier. A man in a dusty black hat, with a full head of hair and a bushy beard, sat by himself with his back to the corner. He wore a dark overcoat, like a duster or a drover's coat, so that he looked like a traveler.

"I don't know," I said. "He's a stranger to me."

The men's singing carried again.

'Twas not very long till she sat by my chair,
She twisted my mustache, she slicked down my hair.

The door of the saloon opened, and a man walked in. He looked our way and lifted his head when he recognized me. As he came our way, Dunbar asked, "Who's this?"

I said, "The clerk in the general store."

Ben stopped at our table and blocked out my view of most of the saloon. "Hey, fellas. What's the news? Mind if I sit down?"

"Go ahead," I said.

He took a seat with his back to the door. After I introduced him to Dunbar, Sloane the proprietor showed up with a bottle and a glass. He poured a drink for Ben and gave me a questioning look.

"Not yet," I said.

Dunbar added, "Me neither."

Ben looked up and smiled. "Put it on my account." As Sloane turned away, Ben gave a simpleton's smile and said, "On account of I got no money 'til payday." He sipped from his drink and said, "What do you think?"

Dunbar shrugged. "I'm here to learn."

"That's why they have these places. Institutions of learning." Ben lifted his glass again.

I waited for him to set down his drink. I said, "Do you know that fellow sitting in the corner behind you?"

Ben turned full around and peered at the man, who stared back.

Ben swiveled back, blinked his eyes a couple of times, and said, "I don't know him. He's a stranger in town."

"Oh," I said.

"He got off the train yesterday and walked into town. Slept in the straw at the livery stable." Ben gave a curt nod to Dunbar and said, "Cheaper that way. Costs two bits."

"One way to do things. Better than sleeping outside. Nights

aren't getting any warmer." Dunbar rotated his glass.

Ben said, "That's for sure. I think it's going to be an early winter."

"Is that right?" said Dunbar.

Ben hunched his shoulders together. "Sometimes you can just tell. I saw a caterpillar with a thick coat of fur. That, and the leaves started turning early. I saw yellow leaves in August."

I said, "I've seen a few. What leaves there are."

Ben moved his head up and down, and with his eyes narrowed he said to Dunbar, "I heard you're lookin' for deer. Well, that's when you find 'em. They come out after the first storm."

"Do you hunt?" asked Dunbar.

"I don't have time. I work six days a week."

Motion caught my eye. The stranger who was sitting in the corner got up and walked toward the bar. As he moved into the light, his features were still in shadow because of his flat-brimmed hat. I couldn't tell if his unkempt hair and beard made him appear more rugged. I had seen men come in after a season in the back country, get a shave and a haircut and a bath, and lose all their rough appearance. At the moment, at least, this man looked as if he had heavy cheekbones, a furrowed brow, and sunken eyes.

At the bar he said something in a raspy voice, and Sloane gave a couple of quick nods. The stranger went back to his table, and Sloane was not far behind with a bottle. He poured a drink, collected, and passed by the table where the four men were singing.

> *She's a dancing young beauty, a rose in full bloom,*
> *And she works for five dollars in the Red-Eye Saloon.*

Ben turned and stared again at the stranger.

"Seems to me I've heard that song before," said Dunbar.

"Oh, yeah," said Ben. "Sometimes it's called the Red Light

Saloon or the Railroad Hotel. And sometimes it's two dollars instead of five." He tipped his head as if he was getting a new look at Dunbar. "They say you're interested in buyin' the Frenchman's Quarry."

"It's just an idea. They come and go. At one point I thought of going into the bicycle business."

"Hah. You won't sell many of 'em here. But you've probably figured that out already. What kind of work have you done up until now?"

"I'm a cowpuncher. That's how I know about sleeping on the ground."

"Oh, well, you can't do that all your life. Punch cows, that is."

Dunbar raised his glass. After he took a sip he said, "Unless you don't live long."

The next day being Sunday, Dunbar proposed to ride out to the Rock Canyon Ranch. He said, "We could visit the marshal when he's at home."

"What for?" I asked.

"Give him a chance to act polite."

"Do you think he's got something hidden out there?"

"Not anything in particular, like a mummy or a trunk of loot. But his hired man didn't seem to want to show us anything more than we had already seen."

"And you want to see how the marshal acts?"

"Something like that. As you know, I'm a sporting man."

"I thought you were a cowpuncher."

He gave me a look with no guile or irony. "I am."

We rode out of town in the middle of the morning. The warm weather was holding constant, and despite the thick fur Ben had seen on a caterpillar, I thought the season of hibernating snakes was still a ways off.

As we rode into the ranch yard, I could see the unfinished stone house farther back. As before, it reminded me of the ruins of a medieval castle or a country church, the types of which one would see in an illustration in a novel by Sir Walter Scott.

The door opened as we dismounted, and Roderick stood in the doorway. He was wearing his star as well as his hat and boots.

"Good morning," I said.

Roderick had an unpleasant expression on his face, not quite a scowl. His voice was flat as he said, "How do you do?"

"Just fine," said Dunbar.

Roderick's eyes came back to me. "What brings you out here on a warm day like this, when you could be sitting in the shade?"

Dunbar spoke again. "The pleasure of seeing the country."

The marshal moistened his lips. "You seem to have been seeing plenty of it." After a few seconds of silence, he said, "What would someone want with that old quarry? All the best stone, or at least the easiest, was taken out of there a long time ago. Not like this place. And it would take a fortune to get it back into production again."

"Oh, that's just an idea," said Dunbar. "What I'm thinkin' about right now is hunting."

"There's no deer here." Roderick had a touch of haughtiness as he lifted his head and said, "And if you're friends with Jum Bailey, you'll find more antelope over that way."

"I'm thinkin' of coyotes." Dunbar poked his cheek out with his tongue.

"Oh, the more of those you kill, the better. But you don't see 'em around here."

Dunbar smiled. "I've seen some good ones along canyons and ravines. Especially on a frosty mornin', on the east side, when the rabbit comes out of his hole in the rocks."

Roderick turned down the corners of his mouth and gave a

small shake of the head. "I just don't see that many coyotes in here. There's better places."

"It wouldn't be for a while anyway. The weather's got to turn cold. Fur's better then."

"I tell Lee to kill one any time he can. That's probably why I don't have many here."

"Oh, I've killed 'em to protect stock, too. But I like a good hide when I can get it. And you know, you can get good hides in poor country."

Roderick looked past us. "Where all are you going today?"

Dunbar took a full breath and squared his shoulders. He spoke in a voice that seemed to have a little more swagger in it. "We thought we'd stop here first, then try a couple of other places."

"Well, there's coyotes out there."

Dunbar wagged his head. "Sure there are. We'll get some." He led his horse out a few steps and ran two gloved fingers beneath the cinch to check it for tightness. Before mounting up he said, "We may come back through when the weather turns cold."

Roderick said, "I'm not always here, but Lee usually is."

I turned the buckskin around, and when I was up in the saddle I touched my hat and said, "So long."

The marshal nodded but did not waste any words on me.

Half a mile out on the plain, I said to Dunbar, "You were right. Give him a chance to be polite, and he takes it. He didn't want to prolong the conversation, though, and he couldn't quite come out and say he didn't want you to hunt."

Dunbar smiled. "That's how it seemed to me. I told him I came out for the pleasure of seeing the country, but it was an equal pleasure to see how he acted."

I decided to reintroduce the question I had asked earlier. "Do you think there's something hidden back in there?"

"Someone's got something they don't want the world to know, but I don't have a specific idea. How about you?"

I glanced back over my shoulder to see the land rising in the distance. "I wonder if it's something they don't want us to see. I've thought about it since we were out here last time, and I remember a story I once heard. Way back in there, past the quarry and the pit, according to legend at least, there's a trail that leads back into a crevice. Sort of a secret passage. It leads out through a split in the rock for I don't know how long. I understand it's wide enough for only one rider, with turns in it that are good for ambushing anyone who follows. Eventually it meets up with a trail that goes through the maze of buttes to the southwest."

"North-south trail," said Dunbar. "I've heard of it. From what I've heard, it's known by horse thieves."

"That would be it. On the other side of where we were looking for deer and antelope." I remembered how Dunbar had climbed up to study the land that day. "You know where I'm talking about, don't you?"

"Yes, I do. I heard of some of these trails when I was working out farther west."

I turned to Dunbar and said, "Do you think it's something that simple, that they don't want us to see a crack in the wall?"

Dunbar shrugged. "Could be that, or the more general idea that you don't let people know or see any more than you have to."

CHAPTER FIVE

Dunbar kept to himself again the next day, going out for a couple of hours in the morning and then holding up in his room for a while. After the midday meal he left again, and when he returned, he went to sit by himself in the back yard. The shadows were beginning to lengthen when I went out to put Pedro on his tether.

"Mind if I join you?" I asked.

"Not at all," said Dunbar. "Glad for the company."

I took a seat in a faded wooden chair. "What's new?" I asked.

"Not much. And yourself?"

I shook my head. "Nothing with me. Just waiting for the weather to change. This weather reminds me of a line from a poem: 'It seems as summer days will never cease.' But of course, they will."

"Oh, yes." Dunbar adjusted his hat. "By the way, you haven't started on the evening meal yet, have you?"

"No, I haven't. Why?"

"Horace is having something like a special event at the café. He's cooking a large roast of beef and intends to serve an evening dinner."

"What's the occasion?"

"He's got entertainment. He says there's a duo of traveling minstrels. Those are his words. They asked if they could play at his place, and he seems to have taken a liking to them. He put the word out, up and down the street in the few businesses that there are, and he hopes to have a gathering."

"This is the first I've heard of it."

"Oh, I told him I'd tell you. Save him the few extra steps of coming this far."

"I suppose if I was more of a butterfly, I would have heard of it sooner."

"I did him the favor of leaving word at the boarding house as well." Dunbar's mustache moved as he rubbed his nose and sniffed. "I didn't mind seeing the inside of that place anyway, just to get an idea of how the other half lived."

"Oh. And where are the minstrels staying?"

"They travel in a wagon. I believe they stay in that."

I reflected for a moment. "It sounds all right to me," I said. "An evening out wouldn't hurt me. What time should we be there?"

"Horace put it at seven. These people will sing for their supper with him and then have time to play a few airs in the saloon."

Dusk was beginning to fall as we walked to the Desert Rose Café. Inside, Horace had lit a candle at each of half a dozen tables, and the aroma of roast beef floated on the air. Dunbar and I were the first patrons, so we had our pick of seats. We sat at a table facing the corner where Horace had cleared a space for the musicians. We set our hats on empty chairs and waited in the quiet room.

Within a few minutes, Ted the barber arrived. He said hello to us and sat by himself at the next table. Shortly after that, Ben the store clerk wandered in, and seeing Ted, he sat at the barber's table. A few long minutes passed, and I found myself hoping that Horace would have a better showing than four customers.

To my relief, Henry Lauck showed up. He was a young man, thin and pale, who worked as a clerk in the bank. People said he hoped to move on to a larger town where he could find a wife and a better position, but in the meanwhile he worked hard and pinched his pennies. When he came into the café, he took off his hat and gave a smile and a nod to the rest of us, then took a table by himself.

Five, I thought. *If only he could get six.*

A shape appeared at the open door, but the person did not come in. I had a pleasant jump in my pulse as I recognized Emilia, waiting, with her hands folded in front of her. She was wearing an everyday dark blue dress, so I assumed she was off work.

I gave her a glance of recognition, and she responded with a brief smile. Then she looked past me.

Dunbar raised his head, nodded, and beckoned for her to come in. As she did, I saw that Lalo was behind her. He moved forward and stood halfway out of sight behind the door frame. He smiled and waved to me, and I returned the silent greeting.

Emilia stopped between my chair and Dunbar's, and he stood up to receive her. She spoke to him in a low voice. "Doña Dolores is not feeling well. She thanks you very much for the invitation, but she cannot go out. She is very sorry."

"So am I," said Dunbar. His eyebrows moved in thought. "Why don't you accept for her?" he said.

"Oh, I couldn't."

"Why not? It's already taken care of. Paid for."

Emilia motioned with her head. "But I have Lalo with me."

Dunbar's face softened as he smiled. "That's all right. He can be my guest as well."

"Oh, no. Thank you, but we couldn't."

"Of course you can. Look. Horace is putting on this nice meal, with good food and music. These people want an audience. And you're done with work for the day, aren't you?"

"Yes, but I must go back and tell the lady that you have

received her message. And after that, Lalo and I go home. Again I thank you, but we cannot."

"Very well," said Dunbar. "Please send the *señora* my best wishes. And on behalf of Mr. Gregor as well."

"I will." Emilia gave me a brief smile again and said, "Good evening." She walked to the door, where Lalo had ducked out of sight, and in a few seconds she was gone.

Dunbar sat down. "Well, I tried."

"Sorry you're out for one ticket," I said. I was sorry also to see Emilia go, but I didn't mention it.

Dunbar said, "A small thing, one ticket. Let's just enjoy the meal and the entertainment."

Much to my surprise, Horace brought out two bottles of wine. He poured it evenly into six small water glasses, then served two glasses to each table. Next he served six plates with generous portions of roast beef, potatoes, and carrots, followed by three plates of sliced bread. He went to the unoccupied place at Henry Lauck's table, raised the glass of wine he had poured for himself, and said, "We can get started." He sat down and became one of the party.

I was paying attention to my meal when the musicians came in through the front door with their instrument cases. I don't know what I expected, but I was surprised to see a man and a woman.

The man wore a brown jacket and a matching high-crowned hat. His white shirt, not quite fresh from the laundry, had a ruffled front with brown bordering, and his ribbon bow tie was chocolate brown as well. The woman had dark blond hair, and like her partner, she wore an outfit that looked as if it had seen some performances since its last laundering. Her dress was dark yellow with flowers and swirls of black brocade, and her vest was of crushed black velvet.

The man brought out a mandolin and played a few notes on

it, and the woman raised a fiddle to her shoulder and applied the bow. The preliminary sounds of music brought a spark of energy to the atmosphere inside the café.

"Good evening," said the man. "I'm Charlie Dan, and this is Betty Louise. We come from Bozeman, Montana. We've been out on a circuit through Idaho and Colorado, and we're on our way back home. Hope to get there before the snow flies. But we've got time to do a few songs for you tonight, some that you've heard before and some that we wrote ourselves. We hope you like it. The first one goes like this right here."

With his mandolin in place, he picked the first few notes of "Red River Valley," and a feeling of togetherness filled the room. A few seconds later, the woman began to sing in a beautiful, plaintive voice.

> *From this valley they say you are going—*
> *We will miss your bright eyes and sweet smile.*

I was caught up, moved beyond anything I would have expected. Hers was the perfect voice for the perfect song, or so I felt at the moment. It seemed as if everyone in the world knew that song and no one would be so deficient as not to feel its beauty.

The song came to a close, and the magic, or the illusion, died down. The woman raised her fiddle, and with a few strokes of her bow she put another familiar melody on the air. The man sang in a steady voice, not deep but rich.

> *I used to have a sweetheart but now I've got none.*
> *Since she's gone and left me I cannot for one.*
> *Since she's gone and left me contented I'll be,*
> *But she loves another one better than me.*
>
> *Green grow the lilacs all sparklin' with dew;*
> *I'm lonely, my darlin', since a-partin' with you,*

73

But by the next meetin' I hope to prove true
And change the green lilacs to the red, white, and
    blue.

The fiddle played on for the space of four lines, and the man joined in again. As before, the room seemed filled with a shared wistful feeling of goodness and sadness, a world in which people thought of lost love and hoped to find it again.

When "Green Grow the Lilacs" had faded away to applause, the man spoke again. He addressed the six of us as if we were a large crowd. "Thanks, fellas. We're glad you like these songs. We sure do. And now we'd like to play one we wrote ourselves. We call it 'Rangeland Lament.' "

He began to play the mandolin in a slow, waltz-like tune, and the woman sang again in her plaintive voice.

Now he sleeps in the cold quiet grassland
Where he used to ride handsome and free,
Just a cowboy who worked for his wages
And on Sundays came calling for me.

Oh he called me his girl of the prairie,
And I called him my knight of the range.
And we fancied the call of the coyote—
Like our love, oh it never would change.

When we walked on the prairie in springtime
We would talk of the years yet to come—
How we'd save for a few head of cattle
And a homestead to call all our own.

We were married the fifth of November
When the wage-work was done for the fall,
And we filed for our land in December,
Plus a brand we could hang on the wall.

For the first year we scratched out a living,
Built a shack and a three-rail corral,
Put a dozen lean cows out to pasture
And were set when the first snowstorm fell.

Of the twelve cows we started in autumn
There were ten that had calves in the spring,
So we planned to have our first branding
When the grass was beginning to green.

But a cold rainy day in late April
Brought an end to the plans we had made
When a trio of men on dark horses
Arrived with the tools of their trade.

From the cabin I heard the shots fired
And his voice as he called me in vain.
Three men in dark hats and dark slickers
Rode away in the cold April rain.

Now the months have gone by, and our cattle
Have been marked with a big outfit's brand,
And with each passing day it is harder
To believe in the justice of man.

When I hear the lone wail of the coyote
At the end of a short winter day
In the thin air of darkening rangeland,
Now his desolate notes seem to say:

Tell me who will mourn for a cowboy
As he sleeps 'neath the cold barren sod—
Tell me who will seek out his killers,
Tell me where is the justice of God?

Tell me who will mourn for a cowboy—
Tell me where is the justice of God?

As the woman sang the final two lines, her voice left a haunting effect, at least on me. As before, I felt transported, but this time into the small, private world of one's own conscience, and I had the sense that each of the others present had looked inward as well. Maybe they didn't. Maybe some of them, like Ted the barber or Ben the store clerk, retreated into the taste of the wine and the roasted meat.

The two musicians knew how to pick up the mood. They launched into a jaunty version of "The Zebra Dun," with Charlie Dan playing the mandolin and singing as Betty Louise tapped out the tune with a stick on a round, hollowed piece of varnished wood.

They played a total of about a dozen songs. When they finished their last number, "Bury Me Not on the Lone Prairie," Horace stood up and called for applause.

"Mighty fine," he said when the applause ended. "These folks need to have their own dinner and catch a little rest. They've got another show, later on tonight. Now, Charlie Dan, if you'll lend me your hat, I'll pass it around."

The rest of us had finished eating, so a relaxed atmosphere prevailed as the hat went around and the musicians put away their instruments. Horace went into the kitchen and came out with two plates of food, which he put on a table in back of us.

Henry was the first to leave, followed by Ben and then Ted. Dunbar and I stood up with our hats in our hands.

Horace thanked us for coming. "I wish more people had come," he said. "But this was all right."

"Very enjoyable," said Dunbar.

I said, "Yes, it was." I turned to the minstrels, who were eating their meal. They looked like everyday people dressed in decorative outfits. "Thanks for the music," I said. "I enjoyed it very much."

"Our pleasure," said Charlie Dan.

Dunbar said, "Good travels."

The duo said, "Thanks" and went back to their meal.

Night had fallen when Dunbar and I walked out onto the sidewalk. The main street was empty, except for a couple of horses tied in front of the saloon, where a patch of light fell from the open door. Most of the other buildings were dark. The tune of the "Rangeland Lament" was running through my head, while the trace of voices carried from the saloon.

Out of the shadows to our left, a man came walking. The light from the café window showed him to be Lee Porter. He nodded to us and walked behind us as he went on his way in the direction of the Diamond Saloon.

A faint breeze kept the night air in motion, not quite a chill but cool enough to remind a person that brisker weather would come. I tensed the muscles of my upper body to get the circulation going as we set off at a direct walk toward my place. We crossed the main street in the middle of the block, coming up onto the sidewalk between the bank and the boarding house.

Dunbar stopped and gave a slow turn. "I don't like that fellow walking behind us," he said. "But he's going into the saloon, so I suppose that's it." Dunbar's mustache moved up and down. "What do you say we take a detour? We can walk past Dolores's house to see if everything is all right there, and we can see if anyone follows us."

"Fine with me," I said. "I could use the exercise to warm up a little."

We crossed the street the same way we had come, and on the other side we walked alongside an empty building to the alley. We turned left, strolled along behind the café, walked another half block, and turned onto the street where Dolores lived. It ran parallel to the main street. After a block and a half, we passed her house, where the light was on in the living room and the shades were drawn. Everything seemed normal and peaceful, so we went back the way we came, ending up again in front of the bank. We headed west again and had just passed the front steps of the boarding house when we heard a shot.

We both stopped. I wondered if a second shot would come, but it didn't.

"Sounds like over by your place," said Dunbar.

"That's what I thought. Let's go the back way."

The moon was not much more than a quarter full, but the sky was clear, so we made our way down the alley without any trouble. When we came to the edge of my property, I was able to make out a dark form on the ground ahead of me, where the back of my lot met the alley.

"That doesn't look good," I said.

Dunbar spoke in a low voice. "No, it doesn't."

We took slower steps toward the shape, which indeed was the body of a person wearing some kind of a dark overcoat. "I'll get a lantern," I said.

Pedro was making commotion in his pen, breathing hard as he moved back and forth and pawed at the dirt. "Whoa, boy," I said. "It's all right. Settle down."

I went into the house the back way, found a lantern, and lit it. I turned up the wick for a brighter glow and went back out to the alley.

Dunbar was standing in the moonlight, his tall hat visible. No one else had come yet.

I held the lantern at waist level so that it shed full light on the body on the ground. I saw at once that it was a man, bearded, lying with one arm beneath him and the other arm outstretched. The sleeve of his coat covered part of his face, but his hat had been knocked off, so that his full head of hair, furrowed brow, heavy cheekbones, and bushy beard made him recognizable.

"It's the fellow we saw the other night in the saloon," I said.

"The stranger in town." The tone of Dunbar's voice gave the impression, once again, that at least some element of this knowledge was already familiar to him.

"This is not a good thing to happen," I said. "Even if someone shot him for a prowler, I don't like it happening right here."

Dunbar knelt, laid the back of his finger against the dead man's brow, and stood up again. He took an audible breath as his chest went up and down. "It's hard to say what happened here or how much. I'll go for the marshal. You can wait here with the light, keep an eye on things. Don't touch anything, of course, and if someone else comes along, don't let him touch anything, either. Looks like that's the man's hat over there. We'll leave it where it is, too."

Dunbar walked away into the night. I stood by myself, holding the lantern and gazing from time to time at the dead man. I felt as if I should be keeping him company, but he was a stranger to me, and I didn't know how I should feel. I got tired of holding the lantern, so I set it on the ground and stood back a couple of yards. After a few more minutes I began to feel a chill, so I walked back and forth to work up some warmth.

Fifteen or twenty minutes passed until Dunbar returned with the marshal.

Roderick stood close to the dead man's arm and gazed downward, with not very much scrutiny, it seemed to me. "Show me some light," he said.

I picked up the lantern and held it so that it cast a full glow on the body. The marshal knelt, tipped his head to either side in a matter-of-fact way, and stood up.

He turned to me and said, "Did you shoot him?"

"Of course I didn't. Dunbar and I were coming back from

the café when we heard the shot. Anyone can tell you we were there for the dinner and program."

"Don't know anything about that. But I don't like someone getting killed in my town."

"It's my town, too, and I don't like someone getting killed in my back yard."

"Who is he?" the marshal asked.

"I don't know," I said. "I believe we saw him the other night in the saloon."

"Which night?"

"Saturday," I said.

"This is Monday."

Everything the marshal said to me seemed to be a challenge or an accusation. I said, "I know."

Dunbar spoke. "The man's been in town for a couple of days at least. I would think that if this is your town, as you say, and you keep your finger on its pulse, you would have heard of him."

"I was at my ranch yesterday. As you well know."

"The same goes for the dinner and entertainment at the Desert Rose Café. I helped Horace spread the word about it. If you didn't know about it, you would have been the only one in town who didn't."

The marshal did not answer him but instead bored into me. "If you don't like someone getting killed in your back yard, that makes two of us. But if you've got an alibi, I'll leave it at that for the time being. I'll go see where I can find Ted."

"I'll stay here," I said.

Roderick gave me a look as if he thought I was the stupidest person in the world. He said, "Well, I should say so." He turned and walked away.

Dunbar stayed with me. After a long minute he said, "Likes to go after all the facts, doesn't he?"

"He never misses a chance to try to bully me."

Dunbar's voice had a droll tone as he remarked, "I should say so."

We stood by the body for another twenty to thirty minutes. I walked back and forth a few times to stay warm, but Dunbar stood in thought with his arms folded. The lantern burned all that time, but nobody else came by. Finally, I heard a sound at the end of the alley, or rather a combination of sounds. Two men were talking, and something was making noise on the ground.

Shapes appeared in the faint moonlight, and after another minute, Ted the barber became visible at the edge of the lamplight. He was pushing a handcart and chatting with the marshal at his side.

Ted slowed down when he came to the body. "This is it, huh?" He turned the cart around and tipped it on its side. He stood up and brushed his hands on his pants. "Unless there's something else you need to do, we can get him into the cart, and I'll take him back to the shop."

"Might as well," said Roderick. He stood back with his hand resting on the butt of his pistol.

Ted bent over. "If you two could give me a hand, we roll him onto the edge here, and then we straighten up the whole thing together."

Dunbar and I rolled the body and Ted maneuvered the cart, and in a few seconds we had everything upright. The marshal tossed the man's hat onto the body.

Dunbar's voice was calm as he said, "We can go back with you, if you don't mind."

"Not at all. There's not much to do at this point, but the light's welcome, and I can always use a hand laying him out."

Ted brushed his hands on his pants again, took hold of the handles on his cart, and got it into motion. I walked at the front of the load, holding the lantern up, as Dunbar walked alongside Ted and made small talk about the weather. The marshal took off at a faster pace, and he disappeared before we reached the end of the alley.

Ted wheeled his cart along, crossing the main street and the cross street, then turning and going on to catch the alley that would lead him to the back door of his business. I held the lantern high as we turned into the area in back of his building.

I knew, as did anyone else in town, that the left door led into the room where Ted took care of dead people, while the right door opened into the room where customers took baths. I held the light as Ted fitted a key into the left door.

He went in, lit a lamp, and came out. I had never been aware that the doorway was wide enough for his cart, but it was, and it all made sense as he grabbed the handles and wheeled his dead freight into the shadowy room.

"Don't put out your light," Dunbar said to me. "I'd like to see what we can while we're in there."

Ted was waiting for us when we went in. My lantern added to the light, and when we got the body laid out on the wooden workbench, it looked more like a dead man than before.

Ted raised his eyebrows as he tipped his head side to side. "Too bad," he said. "But it happens."

"What would you think," said Dunbar with a pause, "of shaving this man?"

"Shaving him? Well, I've done it before, to make a dead man presentable." He gave Dunbar a close look. "It's usually a friend or relative that has me do it, though."

"Oh, I'll pay for it, just as if he was my brother—which he isn't, I assure you. I'd just like to get a better look at him."

"It'll take awhile. I'll have to heat some water."

Dunbar turned to me. "We're not in a hurry, are we?"

"Oh, no," I said. "Not at all."

82

Ted nodded. "I'll get started. He's a little cold already, but that's no trouble. I've shaved 'em in the winter when they've been dead for days." He went out through the door that led to his barbershop.

When the door closed, I looked at Dunbar and said, "What do you make of this?"

"He's cold, all right. I felt that when I first touched him."

"Really?" I said.

"That's right. Colder than he should have been if the shot we heard was the one that killed him."

"Well, well," I said. "That opens a possibility."

"It sure does."

I picked my words. "So it's possible that he wasn't killed in my back yard. Just left there. And the shot we heard was a decoy."

Dunbar gave a short nod. "I think so. And whoever fired it must have thought we had already gotten back from the café." It seemed as if he was about to say something in agreement when a tapping sounded at the back door.

I went to the door and opened it, and there stood Horace.

"What the hell's happened?" The lamplight reflected on his glasses as he looked past me.

"A man's been killed."

"That's what I heard. Who is it?"

"We don't know. It's the stranger who's been around town for a few days." I glanced toward Dunbar and back at Horace. "Ted's going to give him a shave so we can get a better look. He went to heat some water."

"Oh, tell him not to bother. I've got some hot water. A whole kettle full. I'll bring it."

"Go ahead," said Dunbar. "And thanks. I'll tell him."

I was about to close the door as Horace turned away, but he spoke to someone who was out of view. "You stay here." From his tone of voice, I had an idea of who it was.

I held the door open, and Lalo moved into the light.

In a low, confidential tone he said, *"Lo balacearon, ¿verdad?"* Which means, "They put a bullet through him, didn't they?"

"Yes," I said, still in Spanish.

"I want to see."

"Wait. I have to—"

Dunbar came back into the room. "Who's there?"

"Lalo," I said.

"Let him in. Actually, anyone who wants to know has a right to. But we don't want such a crowd that Ted can't do his work."

I stepped aside and said to Lalo, "Come on in. But you have to stay quiet."

Ted came in wearing his apron and carrying a tan crockery shaving mug with the red handle of a brush sticking out. With his other hand he carried a basin, and he had a cloth draped over his forearm. "Nice of Horace," he said. "It'll save time."

Horace came through the door after another minute. He carried a half-gallon teakettle with steam coming out of the spout.

Ted poured about half the water into the basin. He laid the cloth in the steaming water, lifted it out, and spread it over the dead man's lower face. He poured a bit of water into the mug and began to work up a lather.

The back door opened, and Ben the store clerk walked in without ceremony. "What have we got here?" he said in a loud voice.

Ted spoke as the brush clacked in the mug. "Dead man."

"That's what I heard." Ben looked at me. "Did you shoot him?"

I frowned. "No, not at all. Did you?"

"Of course not. I was in the saloon."

Dunbar spoke up. "I think we were all in the café when he was killed."

"That's not what I heard. The marshal said he was killed when you two were on your way back from the café or when you were already there."

"Well, he was already cold. And the marshal hasn't looked close. I think you'll be able to see in the morning that the man wasn't shot there."

"Oh, really? How do you know so much?"

"I don't. And I might be wrong. But I think all the amateur detectives in this town should go there in the morning and look for blood spatters. You know, that's how you can tell if the person was shot in a particular place, and how."

"Sure." Ben pushed out his lower lip, as if in thought. He said, "Why didn't anyone hear the original shot, then?"

Dunbar said, "I don't have any idea of how far away it might have taken place. It's not hard to muffle a shot, though, especially if it is done inside a building."

Ben turned toward the body as Ted lifted the cloth. "That's him, all right. The stranger who was hangin' around." Ben had his head tipped back and his thumbs in his waistband. "They said he'd been lurkin' here and there like a snoop. Up and down the street by Eliot's house, and back in the alley, too. Slept in the livery stable, you know, and he'd go out from there and wander around. Eliot didn't like it and he said so to the marshal. He's got daughters, you know."

"Can't blame him," said Dunbar. "That's the house that used to be the Frenchman's, isn't it?"

"Long time ago, I guess. But it's Eliot's, has been for a while, and he doesn't like strangers hangin' around like that."

Dunbar said, "That's not enough cause to shoot someone, though, is it?"

"No, but who knows what he was doin' somewhere else." Ben looked at me. I stared back at him, and he shrugged. "All I know is what I heard."

I felt like saying, "Then you don't know much," but I held my tongue.

All the time Ben was talking, Ted worked fast. He daubed the lather onto the dead man's beard, then poured more water into the mug and whipped up another batch. When he had the whole beard plastered, he took the razor from the narrow pocket of his apron and began to shave.

He said, "If I had more time, I'd cut off this whole beard with a pair of scissors and then shave the shorter stuff. But the water would get cold, so I'm doin' it the hard way. I'll get it, though."

The five of us watched as the beard was cleared away little by little. Ted shaved and scraped and wiped. He mixed more lather and shaved the whole area again, from the cheekbones to the neck. As he wiped the face a final time, the man's features became clearer. I saw something familiar but couldn't place it.

Ted was swishing his razor in the basin of water. Ben was frowning but not registering any recognition. Horace's eyes were searching.

Lalo's voice came in loud whispers behind us. *"Teem! Teem! Teem!"*

Horace's eyebrows relaxed, and his eyes opened. He said, "By God, it is. It's him."

"Who is it?" asked Ben.

"It's Tim."

Ben shook his head. "I don't know any Tim."

Horace said, "Tim Sexton. The one who got sent up for the death of the little Carreau kid."

Ben shrugged. "I wasn't here then."

"I was." Horace was peering at the clean face. "It's him, all right. He came back, only to end up this way." With his mouth open, Horace let out a short, heavy breath. "I wonder if Dolores knew he was in town."

My eyes met Dunbar's, and I imagined he was thinking the same thing I was. One of the reasons Dolores turned down the dinner invitation might have been that she didn't want to risk crossing paths with the man who had come back to town.

CHAPTER SIX

Dunbar did not have a great deal to say as he sat at the table the next morning. He drank coffee and paid casual attention as I went through the work of fixing breakfast. He watched without speaking as I set the bacon, the hotcakes, the butter, and then the chokecherry syrup in front of him.

"Dig in," I said. "This stuff is best when it's hot."

Dunbar had been staying at my place for more than a week, and although I was still the innkeeper and he was still the guest, we had fallen into an informal style like that of a bunkhouse. I set the food on the table, and he served himself.

He moved his plate next to the small oval platter of bacon and flipped about half the slices onto his own plate. With his thumb and fork together he lifted three of the six hotcakes off the stack.

"The syrup's chokecherry," I said. "When it doesn't jell right, which is about half the time, I use it for syrup."

"That's pretty normal," he said. "Do you make it yourself?"

I moved the butter dish closer to him. "Yes, I do. I go out and get the chokecherries myself, too."

He smiled. "Sort of like gathering stones, but it takes a lot longer. I've picked 'em myself, and I know how long it takes to fill up a bucket." He got some butter onto the knife and slipped it between the second and third hotcake. "I had a fella try to tell me one time that he picked about ten gallons in an hour. I don't know who he thought he was trying to fool." Dunbar reached for more butter. "Not to make light of your own efforts, of course. There's a lot to appreciate when you've done all the work yourself. You've got to boil 'em, mash 'em, squeeze out the juice, and then try your hand at the jelly."

I was glad for the return of his ready conversation. I said, "What kind of a person would say he picked ten gallons of chokecherries in an hour?"

"I'd like to make it interesting and say he was a murderer, but he was just a windbag. I ended up in the same hunting camp with him, and he was full of stories about all the bighorn sheep, mountain lions, moose, and elk he saw every day."

"What were you hunting?"

"Deer. But it was a hot, dry year, and nobody got anything. Not even Nimrod, in spite of everything he said he saw."

"Well," I said, "deer meat goes well alongside this sort of meal. The chokecherry has a bit of a wild taste, and there's something pleasant in the idea that the deer and the chokecherries come from the same kind of country—draws and side canyons and creek banks and the like."

"That's a good way to think of it."

"Just like the rhubarb jam and the hog meat seem to go together."

Dunbar held up the jar of syrup and regarded it. "Dark as deer blood," he said. He poured the purplish-red liquid onto his hotcakes, set the jar down, and moved his bacon away from the overflow on the plate. He said, "No complaint from me about mixing the wild syrup with the hog meat, but I don't care to have syrup on the meat itself. I've seen fellas, like your good old coon hunters, pour that thick, sweet stuff all over their ham or bacon, but I don't care for it."

"Neither do I."

"I must be too much from the North," he said.

This last comment struck me as singular, and it made me realize that Dunbar talked very little about himself or where he came from. His stories more often were about what he had observed in other people.

With a light tone I said, "I take it you don't hunt coons much yourself."

He laughed. "Not much. But our talk makes me think we should go out and get a deer after all. Failing that, maybe an antelope. Earlier I said I didn't know what we'd do with the meat, but it occurs to me that you could use some of it, and Horace could as well. Then there's Emilia and Lalo." He tipped his head and said, "That would just about take care of a deer."

We ate breakfast without saying much. As I poured us each another cup of coffee afterwards, Dunbar spoke.

"Another idea has come to me. What would you think of inviting Horace to have a meal with us?"

"I suppose I could. It would have to be in between his own meals at the café. He just about never takes a day off."

"Maybe a late supper?"

"That would be all right," I said. "Would you like to ask him, or shall I?"

"I'll do it," said Dunbar. "He'll be my guest, you know."

In spite of his casual, unhurried way, Dunbar did not waste time with this latest idea. At midmorning he reported to me that Horace had accepted an invitation for supper that evening.

"I'll go out and get some provisions," I said. Catching his uncertain look, I added, "From the store. I don't go out and shoot supper like Daniel Boone, and I don't gather herbs like the peasants of Normandy or wherever."

His face relaxed into a half-smile. "I feel like a laggard, not having gotten a deer. But we'll work on that."

By early afternoon I had laid in a supply of potatoes, carrots, and onions as well as a fresh chicken. Dunbar showed up as I was getting everything into the Dutch oven.

"I'll tell you what I plan to do," I said. "I've got some oversized chunks of firewood, and I'm going to make a fire in the pit in the back yard. It'll take a couple of hours to burn down to a bed of coals."

"That sounds good," he said. "I'll get something to go along."

He left, and I got the fire started. The odd pieces included the trunks of small trees that would have been too much trouble to split. I had set them aside for an occasion like this, so I was glad to use them.

The fire started at a low blaze. I put Pedro on his stake rope so he could nibble weeds, and I set two chairs near the fire pit. I had just sat down when Dunbar returned with two bottles of beer.

"What, ho!" I said. "A welcome messenger."

He handed me a bottle and took a seat.

"Fire's catching hold," I said. "It should pick up pretty well."

The relaxed atmosphere settled in. The fire made a sound somewhere between a hum and a faint roar, with an occasional crackle. Pedro shuffled his hooves and dragged his rope across the ground. No sounds came from the rest of the town, though it was a weekday afternoon. The sky was a little overcast and a chill hung on the air, but the weather was nothing to keep everyone indoors and silent. I expected to hear something, and at length there came the voice of a woman calling for a child. A couple of minutes later, I heard the sound of a hammer beating on metal. The beer was beginning to relax me, and everything seemed to blend together.

A piece of tree trunk rolled off the fire, raising a little shower of sparks. I used the poker to nudge it back onto the flame.

Dunbar spoke up. "I'm trying to put things together, you know."

"Uh-huh." I settled into my chair and took up my bottle of beer.

"Not meaning to be too inquisitive."

"Go ahead."

"It's too bad about this fellow Tim Sexton."

"Oh, yes. From beginning to end."

Dunbar gazed at the fire, as if he was still picking his words. "You said you were gone when the little boy died and Tim got sent up."

"That's right."

"You said you'd tell me about it someday."

"So I did." I took a deep breath and squinted at the coals. "I guess this is as good a time as any."

"I don't mean to be—"

"No, not at all. I don't like to be one of those people who say, 'I'll tell you something some other time,' and then don't do it. The story's not very complicated, and like I said before, it's no secret. It just doesn't do me much credit."

Dunbar shrugged. "I'm not here to judge you on your past."

"I know." Even as I said it, I realized I had no way of being sure. But I was convinced he was here for something else. I added, "You're too good a chap to ply me with liquor for that. You just want to get the story."

He laughed. "Don't give me too much credit. But you're right. I want to know as much of the story as I can get."

"Well, here's my part. Like I say, it's not much. It goes back twenty-three years, when I was seventeen. I fell in with bad companions, but I don't blame it on them. I wanted more than I saw in this little town, so I went out into the world, or so I thought. These other two were a few years older than I was, and they were a little wiser in those ways that impressed me at the time. They talked about how to live off your wits and make easy money. They knew a place to hold up a train. They invited me to go along and hold the horses. They told me that if anything went wrong they'd keep me out of it, and of course that's not what happened. I got ten years for being an accomplice. During the time I was gone, all this other business happened with Tim and the little Carreau boy, André. When I got out, I came back here to pick up the pieces of this little business. I had plenty of time to think about things when I was in Laramie. The way I saw it, I made a mistake and took my medicine. My mistake was public, and I wasn't one to run from it."

"So you've been back for ten years."

"A little more."

"And, just to get the story, where did your mishap take place?"

"At a little stop called Hermosa, out in the lonesome country south of Laramie, not far from a place called Tie Siding."

"I know those places," said Dunbar. "Pretty country. You can see for miles."

"Yes, it is. I've gone back since then, just to look at the place. Pretty and peaceful. Not that I could appreciate things that well at the time, or see past the end of my nose."

"Part of being young. Not everyone gets the easy lessons."

I let out a weary breath as I stared at the center of the fire. "At least mine was fair. I don't know that Tim's was."

"That's a hard one," said Dunbar. "As for your own story, you say it doesn't do you much credit, but I think it does. You made a mistake and faced up to it. Not everyone can do that."

"Some people make bigger mistakes," I said. "Some of them are still in the penitentiary."

"And others ought to be there." Dunbar raised his eyebrows. "But enough of this dismal talk. Here's Pedro, without a blemish to his soul. It's too bad we can't be like him. A stranger to the malice of man. Granted, he was stirred up by what happened last night, so it's not as if he was oblivious. He could smell death. But evil itself, I don't think it has left its imprint on him."

"He's a good boy," I said.

"Reminds me of a story. Probably an old folktale from the days of the Bremen Town Musicians, but it goes like this. A farmer had an old donkey, and one day the animal fell down into an abandoned well. The farmer had no idea of how to get him out, and after a day or so of fretting, he gave up and decided he would just bury the animal as it was. So he dumped a cartload of dirt down the hole, and then another, and so on. But he couldn't bury the animal. Every time he poured in a load of dirt, the donkey shook his head and climbed up. After a while the farmer realized that if he kept it up, he could get the donkey out of the hole. And he did. So what started out as a little bit of treachery on the farmer's part turned out to be liberation for the donkey. And of course the brute never knew what the farmer's original intention was."

"That's a good story," I said. "It makes you appreciate these animals. Loyal to the end."

The glow of the fire played on Dunbar's face and gave it a faraway expression. "I had a horse die on me once," he said. "It was a cold night, and the horse laid down and couldn't get up. There was nothing I could do, and he seemed to know that. For what it was worth, I said a few words to him, underneath that cold, clear sky. Then I wrapped up in my bedroll, feeling guilty, but there was no other way. In the morning the horse was dead, frost on his muzzle. I took comfort in knowing that he didn't begrudge me."

"I hope I never come to that with Pedro," I said.

"Better not to think about it until you have to."

"That's right. Better to enjoy the fire and the rest of the beer. For which my thanks again, by the way."

Up until that evening, Dunbar and I had taken our meals at the kitchen table, but with the added company I decided to put the dining area to use once again. I had cleaned the room and set out two lamps, so it was well lit when Horace arrived for supper. He was wearing a Scotch cap, a knitted affair with a short wool beak. He took it off and held it in his hand as he and Dunbar took their seats at the table. His wavy grey hair, thinning a bit on top, was tousled, but like his beard, it was trimmed and clean. His blue-grey eyes were clear, and the thin red veins on each side of his nose stood out against his white complexion. His eyes moved to either side, and after seeing how the table was set, he laid his cap on the chair next to him.

"I'll be right back," I said. I went out to fetch the Dutch oven. The coals had burned down and ashed over, and the night was dark, but the oven was still hot where it hung close to the dying coals. I carried it like a bucket, by the bail handle, into the lit dining room. I set it on the table on a wooden board a foot square that I used for that purpose, and an aroma of cooked food drifted with it.

Horace was finishing some small thing he had to say about the weather. He looked at the Dutch oven and said, "It'll be nice to eat someone else's cooking for once."

I said, "You might want to try it before you get too free with your compliments."

"I'm sure it'll be fine." As I lifted the lid on the Dutch oven, he raised his head. "Smells good."

With a roasting fork I lifted the chicken out of the oven and set it on a platter. I said, "We'll let Mr. Dunbar have the honor of carving, if he doesn't mind."

"My pleasure." Dunbar turned the platter and picked up the knife that lay on the table. He took the fork that I handed him, and he paused to study the chicken. Then he went about cutting it up.

I used a metal spoon to serve carrots and potatoes onto each of the three plates. "I'm sorry I don't have any wine," I said. "I just don't keep any on hand."

"Quite all right," said Horace.

I set the spoon on the table. "That was a nice event you put on last night. And the wine went very well with it."

"The event was good as long as it lasted." Horace pushed his glasses up onto the bridge of his nose. "Too bad the evening took such a bad turn later on."

"That was very bad indeed," I said. "Have you heard anything more about how it might have happened?"

Horace shook his head. "No one seems to know anything. Sometimes I wonder why our marshal isn't a little more effective. Here's twice in a little over a week that we've had a death, and it's as if he doesn't want to know anything."

"Oh, I'm sure he does," said Dunbar.

"I am, too, but he lets on otherwise." Horace sniffed. "I don't care for the style. In a small town like this, it's not good when someone wants to keep all the knowledge to himself and treat the rest of us like dunces."

Dunbar used the fork to set a leg and thigh onto Horace's plate. "I imagine he has his reasons."

"Doesn't mean they're good ones. Perfect job on the chicken, by the way."

"Thanks," I said.

Dunbar beckoned for me to hold up my plate as he raised another leg and thigh from the platter.

"And yourself?" I asked.

"I'll have the wings and the back, and then there's plenty on the breastbone for anyone who wants it."

Horace cut his serving of chicken into two pieces. Without looking up, he said, "Back to the marshal. He's made no indication so far that he's taken into consideration what everyone in town knows—that Tim had been dead for a while when you two found him."

"It seems staged to me," I said. "As if someone fired that

shot so we would hear it as we came back from your dinner event. Yet at the same time, it seems as if someone wanted to make it seem as if we had something to do with it."

Horace looked at me and then at Dunbar. "Half a dozen people heard the shot, so there's no question about when it was fired. And Ted himself, who's as much as we've got for a coroner, knows the body was cold. As the British say, this is hard cheese for the marshal. He doesn't like it to be seen that he doesn't know everything, and he damn sure doesn't like to be wrong."

Dunbar spoke up. "How far back do you think that goes?"

Horace's eyes held steady on Dunbar. "You mean with regards to this case."

"Well, yes. I have to admit it's caught my interest. As to whether he was that stubborn when he played marbles or even-odd when he was a kid, I'm not so curious. A psychologist might be." Dunbar gave a wry smile. "Or a phrenologist."

"Stubborn is not a bad word to describe him," said Horace, "though he's more than that. You hear of it in other lawmen. Prosecuting attorneys, too, and judges. They want to have an answer, and they don't want to be proven wrong."

"You mean, they latch onto a solution and don't want to let it go."

"Kind of," said Horace. "They want to solve a crime, yes. But even more than that, in some cases, by no means in all of them, these men want credit for coming up with an answer, which is not the same as a solution. And they want to see someone punished. I see that as something coming from within their own nature."

"And so," said Dunbar, "if that's the nature of their motives, sort of self-centered, as we might say, they have all the more reason not to budge when someone disagrees."

"I think you follow me all right."

"And you think that's what happened in the death of the little Carreau boy?"

Horace nodded. "I think the marshal felt he needed to come up with an answer, he found one, and he followed through. And since then, he's never wavered on it."

Dunbar tore a chicken wing into two pieces and paused. "Do you think he did it because of pressure from Carreau himself?"

"Oh, that contributed, no doubt. It was a big to-do at the time. But Roderick didn't like Carreau, and he wasn't going to do something just to please the Frenchman. I think it was more in the marshal's own character, like I said, of wanting credit for getting an answer and wanting to see someone punished. It's not all authority and appearance, as I see it, though that's a large part of it. It's this drive to punish someone else."

"Even if it's the wrong man," I said.

Horace shrugged. "If you convince yourself that he's the right one, you can go on about your business."

I spoke again. "Has anyone heard how Dolores has taken the news about Tim? I'm sure she's heard it."

"It's got to go rough on her," said Horace. "Her life has been unhappy ever since that little boy died. But I'll say this for her. She's as decent a woman as you're going to meet. Maybe she made a mistake. Like marrying the Frenchman. But all the blame he heaped on her, for not watching the kid, and all the blame she got, just by association when the Frenchman blamed Tim—well, it wasn't fair. She's suffered more than she ever deserved. And I'll say this. As far as I know, she didn't have anything to do with Tim from the time she agreed to marry the Frenchman. Tim took it hard, and he moped around, but she closed things off with him."

Dunbar spoke up. "And you don't think Tim did something to the kid in resentment."

Horace shook his head. "No. I didn't at the time, and I don't now. I think he came back to town to clear his name."

"And to see Dolores?" Dunbar suggested.

"Who knows? He might have hoped to see her, but I doubt she would have agreed to it. Unless it was to make peace with him. After all, the blame fell on him because he was still in love with her, and I'm sure she's never felt good about that. And now this. It just reopens old wounds." Horace shook his head. "No good in any of it."

"Not to mention what happened to Tim," said Dunbar.

"Oh, yes. He lost the most out of all of it." Horace sniffed. "People can die in peace, or they can die in anger, like the Frenchman did, but to die at someone else's hands—there's no justice in that."

"And how about the little boy?" Dunbar pulled meat off the bones of the second chicken wing. "Do you think he died at someone else's hands?"

Horace gazed at the table. "I've never known what to think of that. There was a fellow, name of Dade Flynn, who said he saw Tim go near the boy. But I never liked the color of his ink, and I was glad when he left town."

The talk moved on to other subjects. Horace told a few anecdotes about the earlier days of the town, when all the buildings were occupied and there was movement up and down Main Street. By his account, there were more painted ladies than I recalled, but I would have been a bit young at that time, and he would have been at the age to have a close knowledge of what took place in all the establishments. I had pretty much forgotten about the two saloons on the east end of town, wooden structures with false fronts that had been closed up since before I came back to town. Horace's descriptions of girls with bright eyes and big bubbies made me think I had missed out on something, if only a good show.

The talk came back around to the marshal, Pat Roderick,

and I was reminded of something else I had forgotten. He had been married for a while, but it was during the time I was away, so I had never seen the woman.

Horace told the story in a dry tone. "Roderick went off without telling anyone ahead of time, and he came back with a wife. She was a tight, pinched-looking thing, and she didn't make friends with anyone. They set up in a little house—this was before he bought his ranch—and she wouldn't even go for groceries. She would send her list, and they would deliver the order. In less than a year she was gone, and from what I heard, she got an annulment. People said at the time that it was too bad, because together, they kept only two people unhappy, whereas if they were each married to someone else, they could make four people miserable." Horace shrugged. "Time proves us wrong, though. He's never remarried."

Dunbar, who had been listening to all of Horace's stories with interest, said, "Would this have been before or after the death of the little Carreau boy?"

"Afterwards, by a year or so. It would make a nice theory that he was taking out his misery on Tim, but he had already had the satisfaction of seeing Tim sent up."

The talk drifted on again. We had all finished eating, and the leftover food was cold. I took notice of how well Dunbar had picked all the bones on the wings, back, and ribs of the chicken. He must have seen me observing.

"That was a very good meal," he said.

"Yes, it was," said Horace. "But I have to agree with your earlier comment about the wine."

"Or the lack of it," I said. "My apologies again."

Horace waved his hand. "No need for it. I mention it now because I'm remembering the wine that was left over last night. I think it would be just right if you two would like to go back to my place with me, and we can finish it off."

I looked at Dunbar. "I wouldn't turn it down. How about you?"

"I wouldn't want to be guilty of bad manners," he said.

"Let me put this food away, and we can go."

Dunbar had put on his dark, high-crowned hat and his dark grey vest, and Horace had pulled the beak of his Scotch cap down to the rim of his spectacles. I put on my jacket and my dust-colored hat, and the three of us walked out into the night.

The air was brisk, so we walked at a good pace. A crescent moon, deep yellow against the shaded outline of the rest of the moon, was hanging in the southwest, but the sidewalk was dark in front of the café. When we got there, Dunbar and I stood in silence as Horace bent over and fitted his key into the door. He left the door open as he went inside and lit a lamp. Dunbar and I stepped inside as Horace went into the kitchen area.

A minute later, still wearing his Scotch cap, he appeared with a dark wine bottle in one hand and a tray with three glasses in the other. He stopped short, and his gaze went beyond Dunbar and me.

I turned to see Pat Roderick's hired man, Lee Porter, and a roughneck-looking fellow I had never seen before.

Porter, who had the talent of looking as if he was leaning against a post when there was no post nearby, tipped his head to one side and said, "Seen your light. Thought we could get somethin' to eat."

Horace pursed his lips and said, "I'm not open for business right now."

Porter hung his thumbs on his gunbelt. His right hand held a cigarette. "Well, the door's open, and it looks as if you're about to serve a couple of customers."

"I'm sorry. The door was unlocked, but I'm not open. I don't have a fire in the stove, and I've put all the food away."

"No one said it had to be a hot meal." Porter raised his left hand and gestured with his thumb. "This man has traveled a long way, and there's no other place serving meals at the present."

Horace gave the newcomer an appraising glance. He said, "I wouldn't turn a man from my door. I'll see what I can find."

The stranger spoke in a deep, watery voice. "You don't need to act like it's charity. I pay for what I eat."

I thought Horace would like to tell him to shove off, but it would have been hard to renege at this point. Horace set the bottle and the tray on a table and went to the kitchen.

Dunbar acted oblivious to what I thought was cheeky behavior on the part of both men. In a cheerful tone, Dunbar looked at the stranger and said, "You must be new in town."

"I guess I am."

Lee Porter spoke. "This is Mr. Montgomery. He's come to work as a quarryman."

Dunbar smiled. "For the Bluestone Quarry, no doubt."

"That's right," said Porter. "I came into town to help him get settled."

"And did I catch your name right? Montgomery?"

"You did," said the newcomer. "Yer average fella named Montgomery, he goes by Monty, but they call me Man Mountain."

I had been trying not to pay him much attention, but I had to look at him now. He was a big man, though not much above average height. He had a large head, widest at the ears and cheekbones, with short brown hair and deep-set eyes. He wore a dark blue wool shirt and a shiny brown leather vest with almost a greenish tint. I glanced at his hands and saw large, fleshy mitts with fingers that looked like pale, speckled, uncooked sausages.

Dunbar spoke again in his light tone. "Did you bring tools for tailoring the stone?"

Porter answered. "The boss has a whole tool room of things."

"Oh, I'm sure," said Dunbar. Then turning again to Montgomery, he raised his eyebrows and asked, "Do you drill holes and use dynamite?"

The big man squared his shoulders and tipped his head back. "I'll use what the boss has."

"Might as well," said Dunbar. "I'm interested in all that work myself. Or at least the business of it. Don't know how good I'd be at drillin' and blastin'."

"I do the work." Montgomery spread a smile on his face, showing tobacco-stained teeth. "I leave the business to men with brains."

"Well, I hope you enjoy your stay here."

"Maybe. They say that if you can't have fun makin' the money, you try to have fun spendin' it. But from the looks of it so far, this is kind of a one-horse town. Hard to see where the fun is."

Dunbar shrugged. "I haven't been here that long myself. But I haven't gotten bored."

Montgomery made a small, watery sound in his throat as he said, "I don't suppose there's a good selection of women."

"Probably not like you're used to."

Montgomery's face tightened, but before he could say anything, Horace appeared from the kitchen. He held a plate with four bread-and-meat sandwiches.

He said, "Here's what I've got on hand. I'll ask you to take it with you, so I can close the door. I'd just as soon not have anyone else drop in."

Porter said, "Looks like food to me. How much will it be?"

Horace shook his head. "Nothing tonight. Take it in the spirit of goodwill."

"Are you sure?" said Porter.

"Without a doubt."

"Well, thanks."

"Don't mention it." Horace held the plate forward.

As Porter set one sandwich on top of another, he said, "I'll remember it. Maybe we can do you a kind turn some day."

"Maybe so." Horace held the plate toward the man mountain, who took his two sandwiches and gave an abrupt nod by way of thanks.

When the two men were gone, Horace closed and locked the door. He said, "Let's go to the kitchen, where we can drink this wine with a little dignity. You never know who else might come along."

CHAPTER SEVEN

Among the items left over from the earlier days of the lodging house was a volume of fairy tales by the Brothers Grimm. I remembered the book with its dull, dusty cover, and I thought it was the place where I had first read the story of the Bremen Town Musicians. As I waited for the stove to heat up on the morning after our dinner with Horace, I found the book on the upper shelf of a bookcase in the sitting room. The brown cover was faded with age, and the lettering on the spine was faint. The pages, too, had discolored, but the binding was intact, and I found the story with no trouble. The opening paragraph came alive for me.

> There once was a man who owned a donkey, which had carried his sacks of grain to the mill faithfully for many long years. But the animal's strength began to fail, and he became less and less able to work. His master began to think about how to get rid of him, but the donkey guessed the master's evil intentions, and he ran away. He set out on the road to Bremen. "There," he thought, "I can become a town musician."

I read the paragraph a second time, and a third, and I was in no hurry to read the rest of the story. I might have lingered even more, except that Dunbar came into the kitchen.

"Good morning," I said, surprised to see him that early. "I'm just getting things started."

"Don't let me interrupt anything." He turned a chair to face

105

the stove, and he sat down.

I set the book on the table. "Not at all." I held my hand over the surface of the stove, and I could feel heat coming up. "I hope you don't mind hotcakes again."

"Sounds fine to me."

I set the cast-iron skillet on the stove top and began to make a pot of coffee. "Nice clear morning," I said.

"Yes, it is. I thought it might be a good day to go out and try for a deer. What do you think? Would you care to go along?"

"I'd be glad to," I said. Then a thought passed through my mind. "Would you like to take Pedro along, to carry back the bounty if we get something?"

Dunbar moved his head as if to toss off the suggestion. "Actually, the horse that you ride, the buckskin, is a good packhorse. I talked to the stable man, and we can get a horse for you to ride."

"Oh. When did you talk to him?"

"A little while ago."

"Oh," I said again. I didn't realize Dunbar had left the house and come back already. Now that I looked at him again, I saw where his hat had ridged his hair. "I suppose you'd like to get going as soon as possible."

"No hurry. But some time after breakfast would be good."

I set the coffeepot on the stove top and went to work at mixing the batter. "Did you see anything noteworthy when you went out?"

"No. I'd like to say I saw Man Mountain Montgomery throwing the javelin, but there was no one stirring, not even sweeping the sidewalk in front of a business. Pretty quiet. You'd think nothing ever happened here."

I scattered a spoonful of baking soda across the mound of flour. I said, "After Horace's remarks last night, you wonder how much the marshal knows. More than he lets on, I'm sure."

"No doubt. And I'm sure he counts on people assuming he knows more."

I said, "I think that's part of what I don't like. A kind of smugness. Don't you think?"

Dunbar smoothed his mustache with his open hand. "I guess it depends on what it is that he knows."

I did not carry a rifle or a sidearm for the day, but I did bring along a pair of field glasses, an old bulky set in a thick leather case. I put them in one side of the saddlebags and a canteen in the other. Dunbar was fitted out like a regular plainsman, with his pistol on his hip and his rifle, rope, and canteen tied to his saddle. When I stowed our food in the panniers on his packhorse, I saw more rope, some lightweight canvas sheets, a folding saw, and a hatchet. Dunbar was wearing his charcoal-grey wool vest and a buckskin-colored canvas coat, and he had a brisk, almost animal-like vitality about him. He stood by as I put the food away and climbed into the saddle. Then he positioned his saddle horse, held up the lead rope with his right hand, grabbed the saddle horn with his left, and pulled himself aboard in a smooth motion.

The horse he had arranged for me was a common-looking sorrel. It must have been close to twenty years old, as its back swayed and its ribs were showing. But it stepped out all right with the other two horses, and the sun was not very high by the time we were out on the stony plain.

The sun rose in the sky and warmed the morning, but none too fast. We both wore gloves, and I was glad I had worn a wool coat. I could feel and smell the warmth of my horse, which mingled with the early morning smell of sagebrush, dust, and faint humidity.

We rode for about three hours. The day took on the broad, calm aspect of several of the other days we had seen in the last week and a half. As we got into late morning, I saw very little motion except for an occasional bird of prey gliding in the air currents high overhead.

We came to an area where the rolling plains of grass and sage gave way to foothills. I recognized some of the formations from the day Dunbar and I had ridden out here after visiting with Jum Bailey. I imagined him now, some five miles to the south beneath the sunny sky, beating on a piece of metal in Old Man Harvey's barn.

Dunbar came to a stop and took out his small binoculars. He scanned the country to the northwest. "Over there," he said, with his hand lifted.

I reached into my saddlebags and brought out my own binoculars in the leather case. My horse stood still, with his head lowered, as I brought the field glasses up to my eyes and got them focused. After a little searching, I saw what Dunbar had pointed out.

A mile away, on a gentle slope leading north, half a dozen antelope had bedded down in the grassland. Their colors blended in with the tan and grey of the background, but the dark markings on their heads stood out, at first like specks until I identified the separate animals. They looked very peaceful. A breeze came from the northwest, and I imagined the antelope had found a comfortable lee where the ground rose behind them and absorbed the sun.

I lowered my binoculars. "Did you want to try for one of them?"

"I'd rather find a deer."

We rode on toward the foothills, where dark cedars and bare boulders showed in the ravines. I knew that in this country, the draws and clefts became more numerous than a man would imagine from farther off. In addition to narrow passages that disappeared into the rock mantle, broader canyons could open up out of the earth. We rode into one such canyon, grassy and gentle at first with a cow trail leading down the middle. After a few turns, however, we came to an amphitheater of much greater proportions.

On the left side, which was the northern slope of a ridge, various trees such as alder, pine, and cedar grew thick as in a mountain canyon. In front of us, a rock wall rose up fifty feet to a grassy ledge above. This cliff had layers and striations running diagonally, and at the bottom on the right, a huge, porous, grey boulder stuck out. To the right of this impasse, the canyon continued through a narrow passage almost blocked by a large tree with low branches spreading over a murky pool. Beyond the water hole, the ravine led to a rock bluff about thirty feet high, and beyond, a second bluff that rose another twenty feet.

After we had both looked up and around at the rising walls, I said, "This looks like a genuine box canyon."

Dunbar frowned as he nodded. He was studying the lower levels. "I wouldn't want to be coming down the other way in the dark, or even close to nightfall. It does look as if there's a trail going up through those trees on the left, though."

"Game trail?"

"Cow trail. But I'm always surprised at how narrow and steep a trail those lumbering beasts can get by on. You'd think it's a game trail, except you see cow pies and hoofprints."

"You don't think it would do to go up that way now, do you?"

"Not on horseback. Too many low branches. We can go out the way we came. Is it about time to eat?"

I tipped my head back. The canyon was wide enough that I could see the sun overhead and a little ways to the south. "I think so," I said.

I dug out the bread and cheese and raisins, and we found our separate rocks to sit on. The canyon walls and the rising trees gave the place a feeling of wilderness, in spite of the cow path worn in the grass.

I said, "I imagine some of these places would be pretty good traps if they were under a foot of snow."

Dunbar nodded. "Good places to stay away from in that kind of weather." He smiled. "I worked on a ranch with one fellow who had a story for everything. Whatever kind of country you were in, or whatever kind of work you were doing, he had a story about someone who had come to grief. Got lost in the snow, froze to death, drowned, broke a leg, had the side of his face blown off—no end to it. Snake bites, spider bites, a swarm of hornets, even your barnyard dog that got rabies. Nothin' but disaster and tragedy."

"And he came through it unscathed."

"Pretty much. He had a fingernail that was split in two and grew that way, dark and ugly, and he had a scar on his chin that I don't think came from shaving, but he had all his fingers and toes, both ears, and the tip of his nose—unlike the men in his stories. Not to mention all the ones who died."

"This wasn't the fella who picked chokecherries, was it?"

Dunbar laughed. "No, that fella walked pigeon-toed. The one who had seen a thousand disasters walked with his right foot pointing outward. Both of them would be easy to track if you ever had to."

We finished our lunch and put our canteens away. We tied our coats onto our cantles as well. Dunbar checked the rigging on all three horses, then held his two out of the way as I mounted up. He stepped aboard in his practiced way, and we rode out of the canyon.

Dunbar looked at the sky. "Still early," he said. "They won't come out to graze for another two or three hours, so we might have to look for them where they're holed up."

For the next hour and a half we rode up and down draws and across ridges. Twice we scared up does that bounded away, and

I gathered that Dunbar would rather shoot a buck. We headed north and then made a broad turn to come back south, along a row of sandstone bluffs on our right. Draws and ravines opened up every so often, and at the edge of one of them, Dunbar stopped his horse short.

He swung down and pulled his rifle from the scabbard. He motioned to me, so I dismounted and took the reins of his saddle horse and the lead rope of the packhorse.

In a low voice he said, "Let's go back a little ways. I saw the tail end of two animals, and I want to go up on this side." He pointed to the back side of the ridge.

I held the three horses as he began to take well-placed steps uphill. I wondered what kind of deer, antlered or otherwise, were on the other side of the ridge. I could feel the breeze at my back and the sunshine reflecting off the sandstone on my right. The world was peaceful and quiet. Dunbar moved out of sight, and no sounds came from his movements.

For a short while, perhaps no longer than a minute, I recalled the day I had held the horses at the Hermosa crossing. There had been a different kind of suspense that day. I had stood and fidgeted in the sunlight, with a breeze like this one now. From across a low hill to the west, a lone antelope had come trotting. He stopped and stared at me, with his curved horns dark against the blue sky. He stood there for several minutes, until I heard the rumble of the train and looked away. When I turned back, the antelope was gone. I had thought about him many times, moving free across the rangeland, as I sat behind the walls of the prison in Laramie.

I took a deep breath and brought myself back to the present. There was nothing to dread here. Dunbar either would or would not find a deer to shoot at, and at some point we would ride back into Cantera as free as when we left.

Blam! The crash of a rifle shot rolled out of the draw ahead

John D. Nesbitt

of me. The horses jumped, but I held onto all three as I waited for another shot. None followed. Two does came running into view. At first only their heads were visible, and then the rest of them appeared as they lunged over a low rise and headed away toward the east. Neither of them seemed to be hit, as they both moved at a fast, steady pace. Half a mile away, they dipped out of sight.

I waited for another five minutes, expecting a signal call of some kind, but I heard nothing. Then the horses moved, and I saw Dunbar walking from around the end of the ridge. His stride was relaxed, and he carried the dark rifle at his side.

When he came within speaking range, he said, "We can bring the horses around."

"On foot?" I asked.

"We can ride. They've smelled blood before." Dunbar poked his rifle into the scabbard. As he took his reins he said, "I think it's as much the smell of the wild animal as it is the blood, but it comes to the same."

We rode past the ridge and up the draw a couple of hundred yards. The wheat-colored grass was over a foot tall in the bottom of the draw, and the deer showed as a dark form where it lay.

I dismounted a few yards back and took again the reins and rope of Dunbar's two horses. He rolled up his sleeves and went to work.

He grabbed the deer by the antlers, which had three tines and an eye guard on each side, and dragged the body so that the abdomen sagged downhill. He opened the belly, cutting through the pale underside all the way to the brisket, where the tan hair shaded into darker brown and then the brownish black of the chest.

Dunbar turned the other way and backed up, propping the hind leg of the deer against his own leg. Reaching into the cut

112

he had made, he rolled out the intestines. He shifted position a couple of times, and within a few minutes he had everything cut free. His hands and forearms were crimson as he drew himself up straight, pointed the knife to one side, and took a deep breath.

He said, "It's more work now, but I've got to skin it sooner or later, and I'd rather have the hide off when I quarter this thing."

"Would you like some help?"

"To the extent that you can. If the horses don't give you too much trouble, you could hold up a leg each time."

He cut off the lower legs all the way around, and I held one leg at a time as he skinned the animal on the ground. We tipped the animal one way and another as he worked his knife, and in less than an hour he had the carcass free of the hide.

He held his hands on his hips as he straightened his back and grimaced. "Gets a little tedious, but it's not as bad as skinning a cow. I've had to do a few of those on the ground."

After a minute's rest, he went back to work. He cut each hindquarter out from the hip joint, wrapped it in lightweight canvas, and set it aside. Next he cut away the two shoulders and wrapped them. With the carcass still lying on the hide, he cut out the backstraps and tenderloins and laid them on the wrapped bundles.

"Do you think anyone will want the hide?" he asked.

"I don't know of anyone who would use it."

"We'll just take the horns, then." He opened his folding saw and went to work on the skull. After a few minutes on each cut, he twisted the antlers free and held them out toward me.

"Nice enough to keep," I said.

He set them aside, and after pulling the packhorse away from the other two horses, he began loading the panniers. He put a hindquarter in each side, then did the same with the shoulders and backstraps. He put the tenderloins and folded saw in one side and the hatchet in the other. After a methodical look around, he tied the load snug, and with the last few feet of rope he tied the antlers on top.

"Glad to get that done," he said.

I glanced at the sky. The sun had crossed over but hadn't slipped past the yardarm. "None too soon," I said.

Dunbar rolled down his sleeves and buttoned his cuffs. Some of the blood had worn off as he packed the load, but the backs of his hands were still red. He said, "I wouldn't mind washing my hands at some point, but it's not critical. If we make good time, we should get back to town by dark."

We took a straight route back, stopping once at a windmill to water the horses and let Dunbar clean up. As we expected, we reached the edge of town as the sun was dipping below the hills in the west.

The horses had moved at a good pace all along, so we slowed to let them cool down as we rode into the main street.

Dunbar said, "Let's leave some off with Horace, then some with Emilia, and we'll come back to your place and the stable."

"Good enough," I said.

We passed my lodging house and the empty Emporium building, saw no one on the cross street, and rode on. The light was imperfect with dusk beginning to gather, and at first I did not see the person sitting on the steps of the boarding house. When he stood up, though, I could not miss the shape of Man Mountain Montgomery.

He stood with his arms folded across his chest and a hogleg hanging on his hip. I had not noticed the gun the night before, but I was not surprised to see it on him now. I gave him a nod, and he returned the gesture as he watched us pass.

We pulled up in front of the café, and I stood in the street with the horses as Dunbar went in. A few minutes passed by. I was not thinking about anything in particular when I heard footsteps on the sidewalk. I turned, and looking past the antlers on top of the packhorse, I saw Pat Roderick stepping out of the shadows.

"Got a deer, huh?"

"Dunbar did."

"Where'd he shoot it?"

"Right through the heart and lungs."

I could see his face tighten as he made a small huffing sound. "Always smart," he said. "What I meant, as if you didn't know, was where on the face of the earth he found it."

"In the foothills. A good ten miles west of your place."

"That's what I thought. Like I told him, there's damn few to be found anywhere near my ranch."

Dunbar's voice came up from behind. "And you were right."

Roderick turned and gave no expression. "Lot of work for a little bit of meat."

Dunbar kept a cheerful tone as he said, "Oh, we've got plenty. Enough to share. If you had any prisoners in the jail, we could donate to that cause. Have you arrested anyone?"

"Not lately."

"Saw your new quarryman. Looks like he's at the boarding house, so I'm sure he's taken care of now. As far as food goes."

Roderick's face was still expressionless. "No need to worry yourself."

"Not at all." Dunbar stepped in front of the marshal and began to pick at the lash rope. "Would you care for any of this?"

"Deer meat? No, thanks. I don't care for it. I raise my own beef."

"On your ranch."

Roderick's voice came quick. "What of it?"

"Nothing. Just stating the obvious. I don't know why I do that." Dunbar let the silence hang for a few seconds as he pulled a length of rope to untie a knot. He said, "Then again, some people ignore the obvious. I don't know why they do that."

Roderick's voice was tight. "And I don't know why some people get to be so smart."

Dunbar's words came one at a time. "Maybe they know things." He pulled another knot loose.

"Maybe they ought to stick to things they know. Like in your case, sport hunting."

"In reality," said Dunbar, holding the pannier as it sagged open, "none of this is sport to me. I might have tossed off the term in jest with Owen here, but all of the humor went out of things when we found that dead man in the alley."

"You make it sound as if it's my fault."

"I can't say whose fault it is, but I can say that it's no good to ignore the obvious. The man had been dead for a while when that shot was fired."

"Don't make the mistake of thinking that I'm not aware of it."

Dunbar lifted a hindquarter out of the pannier. "I wouldn't make that mistake," he said. He turned and carried the deer meat into the café.

Roderick walked away without saying anything to me. I hadn't been standing by myself for two minutes when I heard a low, moaning sound like the call of a dove. *Ah-woo-woo. Ah-woo.* I heard footfalls in the street. Turning, I saw Lalo running in his peculiar way with his head forward and his arms down at his side.

He came to a stop about ten yards away and came at me on an arc. In Spanish he said, "They say you got a deer."

"Yes, we did."

He walked past me, still taking exaggerated steps, and sidled up to the packhorse. He raised his hand and ran his finger along the antler beam, then up one tine, and touched the tip. "The man with the fine horses killed it," he said.

"For the meat," I answered, still in Spanish. "We plan to give some to you and your sister."

"And this?" He touched the antler again.

"It belongs to the man who killed it."

Lalo moved his head to each side. "They said you killed a deer."

I was used to his repetition. I said, "Well, we did. Mr. Dunbar killed it. With his rifle. And now he is sharing the meat."

"Was it big?"

"A deer is not as big as a cow. But it is bigger than a goat. Or a sheep."

"Bigger than Pedro?"

"Don't think that way. But, no, smaller than Pedro."

"And the meat is good?"

"You'll see. Mr. Dunbar will give you some, and Emilia will cook it."

"I don't think I'll like it."

"Of course you'll like it. Don't be jealous. Mr. Dunbar is just visiting. You and I will always be friends."

Lalo smiled. "That's right, isn't it?"

A footstep sounded as Dunbar came out of the café. In Spanish he said, "Lalo, how are you?"

Lalo looked down as he scuffed at the dirt. "Well, all right. Just talking to my friend."

"That's good. Well, you know we have a deer. We're going to take some to your sister. Do you go with us?" Dunbar began to gather the rope he had left hanging loose.

"I'll see you there." Lalo turned and took off at his curious run, quiet now. He headed across the street in the direction of the bank, veered right, and ran along the edge of the street until he came to the corner. He turned and went out of sight.

Dunbar finished tying up the pannier. "Shall we go?" he said.

"You'll have to show me where they live."

We mounted up and rode in the direction Lalo had gone. We turned left at the cross street, then right at the next corner. After another block and a half we came to Emilia's house. Light was spilling out the front doorway, and Emilia was standing on the step.

She and Lalo lived in a small, weathered house that looked better in the dusk than it did in daylight. The back street had no sidewalk, so we rode the horses within a couple of yards of where Emilia stood. I made a small wave as we came to a stop, and she smiled as she waved back.

I knew that she took in laundry and pressed clothes for other people in addition to the work she did for Doña Dolores. As she had her hair pinned up and wore a drab dress with her sleeves rolled up above her elbows, I imagined she might have been working.

Her voice was clear in the evening air. "Good evening. Lalo said you were coming."

At that moment I saw him behind her with one hand on the door jamb as he peeked out.

"Yes," I said. "We had some good luck, and Mr. Dunbar would like to offer you some deer meat."

"How nice of him. Thank you, Mr. Dunbar."

He touched his hat and said, "It's my pleasure to be able to."

We got down from our horses, and I took the reins and lead rope as usual. I caught Emilia's eye and smiled. Dunbar began untying the packs, and he set the antlers on the ground near the house.

"I'm going to give you two long pieces," he said. "What we call the loins, or backstraps. It's good meat, with no bones in it." He pulled out one length and held it in the light. "You can cut it across the grain to make small steaks, or you can cut it up into smaller pieces and do whatever you want with it."

"That looks very good."

"If you'd like, I'll carry this in and come back for the other one."

When he had carried in both loins, he rummaged in the panniers and came out with a smaller piece. He brought it forward into the light and said, "Here's something else. This is the tenderloin. It's the most delicate cut out of the whole animal, and I'd like to give it to Doña Dolores." He made a cutting motion with his flat hand. "You cut this across the grain, too. Small pieces. It makes good breakfast meat, or for any other meal. Very tender."

Emilia's eyes followed his movement, and she nodded. He handed her the portion, and as she took it into the house, he leaned over and picked up the antlers.

"And these are for Lalo," he said in Spanish. He held the antlers forward. "If you want them."

Lalo, still halfway hidden by the door frame, said, "I don't know."

"Take them. It's a gift. But don't leave them where the dogs will carry them away."

Lalo took the horns and held them at waist level as he gazed at them. Still in Spanish, he said, "Thank you." Then he held them up to show his sister, who had come back from the kitchen.

She nodded and smiled. With her hands together and a kind expression on her face, she turned to Dunbar and said, "This is very generous of you. We thank you very much."

"Again, it's my pleasure." He stepped back, touched his hat, and turned to the packhorse. He adjusted the load so that the two shoulders were in one side and the hindquarter was in another, and he made a quick job of tying up the packs.

Emilia stood by with the door open to give him light, and I caught her eye again.

When Dunbar was finished tying the load, he said, "We'll go

along, now."

We all said good night, and Emilia closed the door.

As Dunbar and I rode back toward the center of town, I said, "We still have more meat than I know what to do with."

"I've got one other person in mind," he said.

"Not Man Mountain?"

Dunbar laughed. "No, the stable man. If I give him the two front shoulders, he won't charge me for the horse."

"That's a good deal for him."

"More than I led him to expect, but I didn't know how badly I might shoot up something."

The horses walked on in the dusk, their footfalls sounding. I recalled that sunny moment earlier in the day when I had heard one crash of gunfire and nothing more. I could imagine Dunbar concentrating on one clear shot and being satisfied with the results. I glanced at him, riding along with the packhorse in tow, and I believed what he said about none of it being a sport.

CHAPTER EIGHT

Dunbar and I had finished breakfast and were having a cup of coffee when a sharp knock sounded at the door. I got up and went out to the sitting room. As a general rule I did not lock the front door, so all I had to do was turn the handle and pull the door open, which I did in one motion. I was met by the suspended handle of a parasol and the surprised face of Emilia, who gasped. Doña Dolores stood behind her, looking more composed.

"Good morning," I said.

"The lady and I come to visit," said Emilia. She was wearing her housemaid's dress of dark fabric and white trim, and she had the air of being on the job.

I stepped back and to one side. "Please come in. Good morning, Doña Dolores." The words came by themselves, and I hoped I did not seem too familiar.

Dolores gave me a cordial smile as she walked in. She was wearing a grey wool outfit consisting of a full-length skirt, a vest that was buttoned beneath the bosom of an ivory-colored blouse, a jacket, and a shawl. "I hope Mr. Dunbar is here," she said. "The visit would not be complete without him."

"I left him sitting at the kitchen table. Unless he fled at the sound of your voice—oh, here he is."

Dunbar stepped into the room, bowed his head in courtesy, and raised it to let his eyes meet hers. "And a very good morning to you."

"To you as well," she said, giving him her hand.

"This is a pleasant surprise," I said. "Would you like to sit down? Or if you'd like, it's a bit warmer in the dining room. And I have coffee."

Dolores exchanged a glance with Emilia and came back to me. "I think the dining room might do well."

"Let me go first, and I'll light a lamp."

The warmth from the kitchen had come in through the open doorway, and the brass lamp was not cold to the touch as I lit it. Dunbar seated the two women on one side of the table as I went for cups and saucers. As I set them out, Dolores loosened her shawl and let it drape over her shoulders. She did not speak until I came back with the coffee, served all four cups, and sat down.

She said, "I want to begin by thanking Mr. Dunbar for his gracious gift of venison. Emilia cooked some for breakfast, and it was exquisite."

"I'm pleased to know that," said Dunbar.

I smiled at Emilia.

Dolores spoke again, still looking at Dunbar. "I hope I do not presume too much when I say that I appreciate your presence in this town."

"Not at all. And I thank you. But my presence is transitory. It is nothing compared to yours, which gives this town a quality it would never have otherwise."

"Be that as it may. But your presence is an addition that is to be appreciated, as I say, especially in light of certain unsettling incidents that have taken place. There are very few people with whom one can speak with confidence."

"If by unsettling incidents you mean the two recent deaths, I must agree." Dunbar drew his hand down over his mustache. "I can't help think that not enough is being done about them."

"I try to keep those things at a distance, but they do intrude.

What I refer to more specifically is that I feel that someone is watching my house."

Dunbar frowned and said, "Oh. Have you seen anyone you could identify?"

"No. It's always at night, just a shadowy figure that's there and gone."

"That *is* unsettling. How long has it been going on?"

"I've had to think back, and I'd say about seven days."

"And the most recent?"

"Last night."

"I'm sure you have no reason to imagine this," said Dunbar.

"Oh, no. I'm certain I've seen someone."

Dunbar gave a slow shake of the head. "Not meaning to be— well, I have to ask this. Have you mentioned it to the marshal?"

"I don't think it would do much good." Dolores drew a full breath. "And furthermore, as a general practice, I do not speak to him." This last statement had a definitive tone to it.

Dunbar nodded. "Even those who do speak to him are not likely to get much for their trouble."

Dolores did not offer a response.

"Back to the topic at hand," said Dunbar. "If you think you saw someone as recently as last night, then it wouldn't have been Tim Sexton, though he might have been a likely suspect a couple of nights earlier and for a few nights before that."

A stiff pallor seemed to take over Dolores's face.

"I'm sorry for the mention of something disagreeable," said Dunbar. "I'm just trying to cover possibilities. But perhaps you have something else in mind."

"Perhaps."

Dunbar relaxed his gaze and glanced around the table. "Well, we're all friends here, so please speak as free as you wish."

Dolores had her hands in her lap, and she had not touched her coffee. She said, "Mr. Dunbar, again I hope that I do not presume too much when I say that I think you could be of help to me."

His eyebrows moved, but his voice was calm as he said, "It might be beneficial to me as well, depending on what you need."

After what seemed like a deliberate pause she said, "I would like to know who is spying on me, and if it is possible, I would like to make him quit."

"That's clearly stated."

"And I'm willing to pay you for your work."

Dunbar shook his head. "I don't hire out for that sort of thing. But that doesn't mean I wouldn't do it."

Dolores's eyes tensed as her eyebrows went up. "I wouldn't want to owe anyone a favor."

"You wouldn't. Not if you helped me in return."

Dolores took in a slow breath. "In what way?"

"At the risk of touching on another subject you would rather not discuss, but in the spirit of stating things clearly, I'll say this. I've become interested in knowing more about the death of little André."

Dolores became rigid and pale again, though even more so, and for a few seconds she looked as if she could have been a pillar of salt. At length she said, "You are right. That is a painful subject for me to discuss."

"I understand."

She looked at him as if she didn't think he did, but the tone of her voice indicated that the hard part of the conversation was past. "I'll consider it," she said.

"I couldn't ask for more. And if I get a chance, I'll wander by there a time or two this evening."

She smiled. "I'll try not to mistake you."

He laughed. "And with that, too, I couldn't ask for more."

I had already decided to spend part of the day working with the deer meat, so when the visitors were gone and I had everything picked up, I brought in the hindquarter from where I had left it hanging the night before. It had cooled well and was in no danger of spoiling, but there was quite a bit of meat, and I wanted to make good use of it.

First I cut out the bone, which did not take long. Now I had a large hindquarter of pure meat. I cut off the shank end and then an uneven piece on the hip end. I trimmed the fat from the irregular piece, and seeing how much I had now, I cut it and the shank meat into chunks for the stew. I put the cut-up meat into a large skillet to cook first, as I had learned long ago that wild meat lost some of its strong taste if it was cooked in an open pan.

Following the natural divisions of the muscles, I separated one large piece from the rest of the remaining hindquarter. It would have made a five-pound roast or a half-dozen steaks, but I still had plenty of meat for that, so I went to work cutting this piece into strips for jerky.

As I worked, I had recurring thoughts about Dolores's visit earlier in the day. I felt a lingering sense of her presence, a strange blend of her feminine charm and natural grace being muted, or rather stifled, by some force stronger than sadness alone. Pain, sadness, guilt—it seemed all of these and more, inseparable, and it seemed always to haunt her.

And there was Dunbar, gallant and accommodating. If he had not been ten years her junior, and if she had not had her aura of sorrow, I might have thought there was an attraction developing. Instead, I felt as if their spirits met on a higher plane, where age and one's station in life did not matter, but where there was a kind of courtship for truth—uncertain like other courtships, with one person advancing and the other resisting, demurring, delaying. And unlike youthly courtships, this one seemed fated, if not by time, then by truth itself.

I did not have to invent these melancholy feelings. They hovered in the air. I was glad to get all the meat sliced and seasoned and laid out on wire racks. Next I poured about a gallon and a half of water into the stew pot, cut up some carrots and potatoes, and put them in along with the pan-fried meat. The water would take time to heat, so I tended to a couple of other things. I took the leg and thigh bone, one hinged piece, out to the alley and left it for a dog to find. I said hello to Pedro and went back into the dining room, where I had found half a dozen hard biscuits wrapped in a towel. These I took out to Pedro and gave to him, one by one. The biscuits were rock-hard, and as always I was impressed by how much force he had in his jaws. His muscles worked from his jawbone up across his temple and his heavy brow, and little by little he ate each biscuit. I gazed at his broad, woolly forehead with its cowlick curl, and I wondered what thoughts, if any, transpired inside.

Dunbar had come and gone in his usual unannounced way. At a little after noon he came into the kitchen, where the stew was simmering.

"Good things in the air," he said.

"I've got stew cooking, but it won't be ready until later on. There's bread and cheese for right now, and we can have the evening meal whenever we want. Any time after five, I'd say."

"That should be fine. I got my sheets of canvas back, and I'd like to wash them and hang them out to dry. Yours, too, if it's convenient. Then at some time after dark I think I'll take my first round to see if someone's lurking in Dolores's neighborhood."

"What do you think?"

"I have no reason to doubt her. As for who might be peeping, my first suspicion would be the new man in town, Mr. Montgomery, but she says it's been going on longer than that. By her time frame, it would seem as if someone was watching to see if Philip Gaston and then Tim Sexton had come to see her at a less-public hour, but if that was the case, I don't know why someone would still be watching. Nor do I know why someone would be concerned if either of those two men spoke with her to begin with. But that goes along with other things yet to be explained." Dunbar shrugged. "It's all kind of dubious, but you asked me what I think."

"Oh, well, just making conversation."

"No harm in that."

Darkness came, and the four canvas sheets hanging ghostlike on the line were still damp to the touch. Pedro also looked like a ghost, as I could see only the grey area around his eyes and on his muzzle. From a side view I saw the greyish-white bottom of his belly.

I went inside and stirred the stew. The carrots and potatoes were cooked, and the piece of meat I sampled was tender. Warmth from the stove had spread through the dining room and the front room. It would have been a suitable time for company. I imagined Dolores and Emilia coming again to visit, taking off their gloves and wraps, and sitting down. I told myself it would be a good idea to have on hand a wine or other cordial. Then I realized how unlikely it would be for those women to make a social call. Dolores would not have visited the first time if she were not looking for something like a bodyguard, and Emilia would not think of coming on her own. Still, it was not a bad thought.

Dunbar did not come in until well after dark, and he did not have his cheerful demeanor. "I'm not sure how to go about this," he said, "but I think we should go see Emilia."

"Is something up?"

"I can't tell. I watched Dolores's house from one vantage point and another, until I thought someone might take me for a lurker. A light was burning in the parlor, but I didn't see any movement in the house—no passing shadows, no lights in other rooms—and I thought the one light grew a little dimmer. Just before I left, I knocked on the door. No one answered. The door was locked, which was just as well. I'd rather not go in by myself."

"So you'd like to call on Emilia."

"She could let us in. If Dolores is just not answering the door, that's all right. If she needs something, we're there to-gether."

I considered what he left unsaid. Nodding, I said, "Sounds like the best course. Would you like to eat something first?"

"Not really."

"Well, let me take the pot off the stove. I'll get my hat and coat, and we can go."

We went out into the cold night air, which seemed heavier than it had been for the past few evenings. I wondered if humid-ity was moving in to bring another spell of clammy weather.

Emilia answered the door at the first knock, and her expres-sion of surprise changed to one of worry as Dunbar told her of the situation.

"Just a minute," she said. She closed the door, and her footsteps went away. I heard her say a few words in Spanish in the tone she used with Lalo. Her footsteps came back, and the door opened. She was wearing a wool jacket and carrying a ring of keys.

We walked the four blocks to Dolores's house without speak-ing. A dim light was glowing in the front room. The curtains were drawn, but that was almost always the case at that house.

Dunbar and I waited as Emilia unlocked the front door and

pushed it open a few inches. As she jiggled the key to take it out, she looked over her shoulder and said, "Come in."

We stepped inside, and I closed the door as Emilia crossed the room to turn up the lamp. The upholstered red chairs brightened in the improved light.

"*Señora,*" Emilia called out. "*Señora. Aquí venimos. Están conmigo los señores.*" My lady. We are here. The gentlemen are with me.

No answer came. The door to Dolores's office or study, where she had visited with Dunbar on our earlier visit, was ajar.

"Can we light another lamp and look around?" Dunbar asked.

"Yes. Of course." Emilia went to a sideboard where another lamp sat. She struck a match, lifted the lens, and lit the wick. After a few seconds, a glow of light spread out.

She carried the lamp to Dunbar and handed it to him. He held it at chest level and approached the door to the study. With the backs of his fingers he rapped on the panel of the door.

"*Señora.*" His voice was calm and steady, not loud. "*Doña Dolores.*"

He pushed the door open, and light flowed into the room. I stood behind him and to one side, and Emilia stood behind me. My eyes scanned the room and came back to the desk that sat in the middle and faced the door. The room seemed empty, or at least unoccupied, but I knew it was Dolores's room, and I did not like the feeling of trespassing.

Dunbar, too, had held up, pausing at the threshold. Then he moved to the desk, set the lamp on the back corner, and knelt. Emilia rushed in behind him, so I was the third one to see what was on the floor behind the desk.

Doña Dolores lay in a prone position, full length, with her head turned to the left and her dark hair with threads of grey covering most of her face. Her right arm was tucked beneath her, and her left arm was reaching out, bent at the elbow, as if she were asleep.

Dunbar touched the side of his finger on her neck. He shook his head. "I'm afraid it's too late. She's been here awhile."

Emilia let out a sob and began to cry. *"Señora, señora, señora. Que Dios le ayude."* May God help you.

Dunbar stood up. "This is no good. Worse." He looked past me. "Somebody has got to go for the marshal. Of all things. Somebody should stay here, too." He moved his eyes back to the body and to Emilia, who was kneeling and praying. I do not know the specific words, but the soft, rhythmic sounds are unmistakable.

"I can go or stay," I said.

"Let's see." Dunbar knelt and put his arm around Emilia. "I am very sorry," he said. "This is a terrible thing, but someone has to go for the marshal. One of us will stay here. I don't know if you want to stay or go home."

"I will stay with the lady."

"Very well." Dunbar patted her on the shoulder and stood up. His eyes were sad as he turned to me. "What would you think of going for the marshal?"

"I can do it. But what if I can't find him? What if he's gone to his ranch?"

"He should be in town. My understanding is that he goes to his ranch on Sunday. But if he's gone, I suppose it can wait till morning. No sense breaking your neck going out there in the dark. We wouldn't move the body until morning anyway, and I'm sure Emilia will want to sit up with it all night."

"I'll see what I can do." I realized I hadn't taken off my hat, so I took it off as I moved a couple of steps and looked down. My eyes brimmed with tears as I said, "I'm sorry, Doña Dolores. May God be with you."

I put on my hat and went out into the night. I found the jail dark and locked up. I backtracked to the saloon, poked my head in, but said nothing. After taking a deep breath, I went to the boarding house and asked for the marshal there.

Hicks, the proprietor, did not ever waste any friendship on me, but he showed interest now. He said, "The marshal's not here. I believe he's gone to his ranch. But if you'd like to leave a message, I can be sure he gets it as soon as he's back in town."

"Thanks," I said. "It can wait."

I went out into the night and walked back to Dolores's house, where I joined Emilia and Dunbar. Emilia was sitting in the office chair, not a foot away from her beloved lady. Dunbar was on his feet with his hat in his hand, and I guessed he had been pacing. When I told him the marshal was out of town, he shrugged.

"I guess we wait, then." He motioned with his arm toward the two red chairs.

We hung our hats on the hall tree and took our seats. I could hear Emilia murmuring as I crossed my arms and settled in for the long vigil until dawn.

Grey light had crept into the room. I realized I had dozed off. Someone had turned off the lamp in the front room, and the office lay in darkness. Dunbar's chair was empty.

I got up and crossed the room. As I peered into the office, I could make out the form of Emilia, still sitting up but with her head tipped to the side as she slept. I went back to sit in my chair.

A few minutes later, the front door opened and Dunbar came in. He said, "No sign of the marshal yet. Of course, it's still early. I couldn't sleep. I got restless." He sat down.

A sound came from the office, and Emilia appeared in the doorway. She looked weary but not exhausted, and I imagined she had found strength in her prayers. She said, "I'll make some coffee. And you'll want breakfast."

Dunbar rose to his feet. "I can do it," he said. "If you'd like, you can stay with—"

"She is with God. Please sit down, and I will make breakfast. It won't be long." She left the room by another door, and Dunbar sat down again.

Time dragged on. I heard the sounds of Emilia building a fire in the stove, setting pots and pans on the solid iron top, and cutting food on a board. Dunbar got up and paced back and forth.

He stopped, and without any preamble he said, "I think it would be best to keep the body here. It's the way many of these people do things anyway. I don't think Emilia will mind staying here. We'll send for a priest, and I'll find out what I can about family members. The marshal has to get in here, probably with Ted, to determine the cause of death, but I'd like to keep his hands off of things as much as possible. Keeping this house occupied is a good idea, I think."

Emilia came from the kitchen to call us for breakfast, and we followed her to a small, neat dining area. As we sat down, she served us each a plate of fried potatoes, eggs, and meat. With a sense of incongruity I realized she had cooked the last of the deer tenderloin.

"I feel that we're imposing," I said.

Emilia shook her head. "Not at all. *La señora* would not want this food to go to waste. As she would say, *sagrados alimentos.*"

Blessed food. Dunbar and I ate without further resistance. After a cup of coffee, I offered to go out again and look for the marshal.

The sun had risen, but a chill lay on the air. I walked to the main street and headed west in the direction of the jail. I glanced across the street at the general store, where a rack of brooms on the sidewalk indicated that the store was open for business. I imagined Ben the clerk had started his day. Perhaps heavy-lidded Ross Ferguson was at his desk as well. Life went on, and Doña Dolores would never see any of it again.

The door opened, and a person came out of the store. As he walked to the edge of the sidewalk and stood in the sunlight, my pulse jumped. It was Pat Roderick. He waved for me to come over.

I crossed the street, and when I was within a couple of yards of him, his voice sounded in the empty morning.

"I heard you were looking for me. What do you want?"

I had my line rehearsed, but I had to take a breath and work myself up to it. "There's been a death at Dolores Carreau's house."

He gave no expression at all. "Inside or outside?"

"Inside."

"Anyone you know?"

"It's Dolores herself."

Roderick heaved a breath out his nose and gave an impatient drop of his chest and shoulders. "You little rat. Why do you have to play games?"

"I was answering your questions."

"Son of a bitch." He stepped off the sidewalk. "I'd better go take a look. Is the body still there?"

"No one has touched it. At least since we found it."

He said no more, and he ignored me, as he liked to do, as we walked the two-and-a-half blocks to Dolores's house. Emilia let us in, and the marshal's face stiffened as Dunbar came forward.

"Where's the body?" Roderick asked.

Dunbar motioned with his hand. "In there. In her office."

The marshal walked in, and I followed him as far as the doorway. He cast a cold glance at the floor where Dolores lay, and his eyes swept the area a couple of times. He squatted, tipping his head to one side, and after a minute he stood up. He

133

was still wearing his hat, and he showed no emotion as he turned.

"No telling how she died, just on the face of it. We'll have to get Ted. Maybe you two can help him."

Dunbar had come up beside me. In a calm voice he said, "I think we can leave the body here."

Roderick's face went hard. "What do you mean?"

"I talked to Emilia about it. There's a divan in the next room, and we can lay her out there until a priest gets here. Meanwhile, we'll notify her family. I understand she has a sister."

Roderick's face muscles moved. "Don't take too much on yourself. I'm the law here."

"Not by much," said Dunbar. "For as little as you do."

A flush rose on the marshal's neck, colored his ears, and tinged his face. "Don't give me trouble," he said, "or I'll arrest you on suspicion."

"You'll do no such thing. The three of us found her together. If you think she died under suspicious circumstances, you need to arrive at that finding. You can bring Ted here, but unless you can prove otherwise, Mrs. Carreau died at home just as a great many people do, and their families take care of them for burial."

Roderick seemed ready to burst with anger, but he kept control of himself. His eyes moved from Dunbar to me as he said, "I'd like to see both of you in jail for some of these things."

Dunbar raised his brows. "Like you did with Tim Sexton?"

Spit flew from Roderick's lips. "Don't push me," he said. "You'll be sorry you did."

Ted came and went, and we moved Dolores to a narrow couch in what served as a spare room. It was on the shady side of the home at this time of year, and the other objects in the room were cold to the touch. Emilia opened two windows for cross-ventilation, and cool air flowed in.

By now it was midmorning. Dunbar said he would go to the telegraph office and send for a priest. He had gotten the name of Dolores's sister from Emilia, and he said he would send for her as well.

I walked with him out to the front step. "What do you think the marshal will do?" I asked.

"Not much, in spite of his bluster. I think he and Ted will find she died of unknown, if not natural, causes."

"You don't think he'll want to investigate?"

Dunbar shook his head. "Not any more than he has done in these other cases of late."

"You don't think he'd like to hang it on one of us?"

"He knows better."

Shortly after Dunbar left, Horace knocked on the door. As Emilia let him in, he took off his cap and sniffled. He shook his head and said, "I can't believe she died. There was nothing wrong with her. She was still young—not as young as she once was, and she had seen her troubles, but she was not old." He turned to Emilia, who had closed the door. "I am very sorry," he said. "I know you cared very much for her. We all did. She was a beautiful lady."

Tears came to Emilia's eyes again. "She is with God. Would you like to spend a few minutes? She is in the next room."

Horace nodded as he folded and twisted his cap in his hands. "I'd like to pay my respects."

I sat in my chair as he made his visit. Emilia went to the kitchen. After about ten minutes, Horace came out. I got up and took a couple of steps forward. He stood close and spoke in a quiet voice.

"The word is that she died of natural causes."

"Is that what the marshal said?"

Horace blinked as he nodded. "He and Ted both. I find it hard to believe. There was nothing wrong with her. But I don't know why anyone would want to do anything to her."

I shook my head. "Neither do I."

"She wasn't that old. I'm old, and I don't have one foot in the grave yet. At least I hope not." Horace held his blue-grey eyes on me. "I wish someone could find out something."

"So do I. Dunbar is sending for her sister. No telling whether she knows anything." I wasn't sure of how much I should say, but I went ahead. "Even if she doesn't, I think Dunbar will do something."

CHAPTER NINE

The priest sent word that he would arrive early on Saturday and would have to leave later the same day, as he had a marriage to perform on Sunday in Glenrock. Dolores had died on Thursday evening, and her sister had sent a telegram saying she would arrive on Wednesday or Thursday of the next week, so having the burial on Saturday seemed like the best thing to do.

Horace and I talked to Ross Ferguson, who was the owner of the one church building in town. At an earlier time there had been three churches in Cantera, all of them wooden structures, but two of them had fallen into disuse. The one that survived lay on the east edge of town, on a corner by itself. It became the Presbyterian Church on Sunday morning and the Methodist Church on Sunday afternoon. At other times it served other purposes, such as the present one, when a clergyman from another religion came through.

On Saturday, Dunbar hired a carriage and fetched the priest from the train stop. Meanwhile, Ted came to Dolores's house with his horse and wagon, bearing a grey, cloth-covered coffin. He and I carried it into the house and got the body settled into the scant padding. Emilia had done a good job of preparing the body. Dolores looked calm and at rest, with her face powdered and her lips colored. I could only wonder at what information she took with her, and I felt a twinge of guilt as I hoped her sister would bring some knowledge when she came.

Ross Ferguson arrived with his clerk, Ben, and the four of us carried the coffin out to the wagon. Ferguson rode on the wagon seat with Ted while Ben and I followed for three blocks on foot. We unloaded the casket and took it into the church.

I was standing around inside, idle, with my hat in my hands when I saw a carriage through the open door. I went out to meet the priest. He was a small man sitting next to Dunbar. In contrast with Dunbar's buckskin-colored coat and tall black range rider's hat, the priest was wrapped in a dark traveler's overcoat and topped off with a short stovepipe hat. He wore spectacles and had a florid face, but he had the weathered texture and the seasoned expression of a man who had traveled a great deal and seen his share. If he hadn't been wearing his priest's collar, I might have taken him for a horse trader or a medicine salesman.

He picked up his traveling bag and held it at his hip as he stepped down from the carriage. As he gave me his firm hand to shake, he introduced himself.

"I'm Father Caldwell. Come to bring comfort in this time of sorrow."

I said, "Thank you for coming, Father. We appreciate it."

"I come of God's will." He raised his chin, hefted his bag, and headed for the door of the church.

I lingered in the sunlight as Dunbar moved the carriage and tied the horse next to Ted's. When I went inside a few minutes later, Father Caldwell had put on a cassock and had set out a small silver pitcher, a chalice, a tray with tablets of communion bread, two candles, and a silver cross with a rosary draped on it. He took out a silver watch and consulted it.

"Set for eleven, isn't it?"

"Yes," I said. "People should be here pretty soon. I don't know how many will come, but I don't expect a great number."

He nodded and turned away. From his bag he took out a Bible with a soft black leather cover. With one hand holding the drooping book and the other curved like a little paw, he turned the thin pages several at a time until he came to a stop. His spectacles moved as he scanned the text. Then he took the rosary from the silver cross, laid it for a bookmark, and held the Bible open as he moved to the casket and stood next to it.

People began to arrive with muffled sounds. I took a seat toward the back, but before long I moved up a couple of rows. I counted the people present and noted who had come. Emilia and Lalo sat in front, closest to the casket. On the other side of the aisle sat Horace, Dunbar, and Ross Ferguson. Behind them were Ben, the store clerk; Henry Lauck, the bank clerk; and Jim Sloane, the saloon owner. Two rows behind Emilia, Jess Fluornoy, the stable man, sat by himself, and across the aisle from him sat Ted, the barber and undertaker in one person. There were a dozen in all, including the priest. I made myself not think of the people who did not come.

The priest had his hands raised out from his body, palms upward. His voice rose in an oratorical tone as he recited a long sentence in Latin. After this invocation he proceeded to conduct the service sometimes in Latin and sometimes in English. Emilia, Lalo, and Jess Fluornoy knew when to kneel, when to sit on the bench, and when to recite. The three of them went up for communion, and in less than an hour the service was concluded.

Ted designated Horace, Ross Ferguson, Ben, Henry, Dunbar, and me to be the pallbearers, and he led the way to the wagon. From there we made a small procession with the wagon, the carriage, and eight of us on foot. A cool breeze came out of the northwest, and the sun at midday lent a bit of warmth.

The cemetery lay south of town, about a half-mile out. Ted had prepared the grave where Pierre Carreau had assigned it in the family plot before his death. As one faced the headstones, André's was farthest to the left, then Angélique's, then Pierre's.

Dolores's grave came next, with the headstone in place but the date of death yet to be etched in. Farther to the right, the mound of dirt was covered by a sheet of canvas.

The same six of us as pallbearers lifted the casket from the wagon and carried it to the foot of the grave. There we gathered around it without standing on anyone else's space, and the priest said a few more words as he commended Dolores to God's mercy and kindness. Ted had ropes at hand, and four of us lowered the casket. The priest scattered a handful of dust, and after a few seconds of silence he said, "We have done all we can at the moment. Let us pray for Dolores, each in our own way, and let us go in peace."

Emilia said to Lalo, *"Un puño de tierra."* Each of them took a handful of dirt from the mound and sprinkled it on the casket.

Then we went in peace, as the priest said, leaving Dolores in her final resting place. I thought the four people buried there made an odd family, all together again, and I wondered what life had been like when they had been alive together.

Father Caldwell stayed long enough to eat dinner with the rest of us at Horace's café. It was a quiet, somber event. Afterwards, Dunbar drove the priest to the train stop, and I walked with Emilia and Lalo to their house. We paused at the front step.

"Mala estrella," said Lalo, sniffling. A bad star.

Emilia's voice was choked as she said, *"No hay remedio. Que en paz descanse."* There is nothing we can do. May she rest in peace.

I gave each of them a hug and went on my way. I walked back toward the lodging house by way of the main street. Two range riders, in town on Saturday, walked into Horace's Desert Rose Café. A cat came out from behind the next building on my left, then turned and darted back. Through the barbershop window I saw Ted sitting in his barber chair, talking to Hicks, the boarding house proprietor, who sat in a wooden chair with his arms folded. Ted waved to me.

Across the street, the stone bank reflected the sunlight of early afternoon. The glint of the front door moved as Eliot, the banker, stepped outside and locked the door behind him. From a block away, beyond the bank and the boarding house, came the crowing of a rooster. I thought of Dolores lying in the dark ground, and I took a deep breath to hold back the emotion. I recalled Lalo's phrase about a bad star and then Emilia's simple but true expression. Emilia was right. There was nothing we could do about it. Around me, in the thin, warming afternoon, life went on in Cantera.

Dunbar came in a while later and went to his room. He emerged a couple of hours later as I was chunking up a fire for the evening meal.

"Sad day," I said.

He turned a chair around and sat down. "Yes, it is. I'm not much for funerals, but it would have been out of the question to miss this one."

"Certainly the case with me. You would have thought more people from town would have gone to it, but Doña Dolores kept to herself quite a bit, and anyone who had come to town in the last several years would hardly have known her." I took a breath and continued. "But, as they say, the funeral is for those who are there, and I think we did justice to her in that respect."

"In that respect," he said.

"Oh, I know. I don't believe for a minute that the other justice is done. Nor do I believe that she died of natural causes. What do you think?"

Dunbar's mustache moved as he twisted his mouth. "Like I said when that young fellow Gaston met his end. I think someone might have a jar of chloroform. Whoever it is, I'm sure he keeps it well hidden. Ted would be the closest source of something like that, what with the nearest apothecary or druggist nearly a day's ride away, but I doubt that he would know anything about it. Someone who wanted such a thing for those purposes would not want anyone close by to know he had it."

"It's pretty common stuff," I said. "Any amateur entomologist is likely to have a bottle of it."

"Oh, yes. It's just a matter of what you do with it. Like rat poison, or cockroach poison, or any of them. Arsenic, strychnine, nitroglycerin."

"Nitroglycerin? I thought that was an explosive."

"It is, but it's poisonous as well. All in how you use it. But enough of this cheerful talk. I'll tell you, I think we should drop in on Horace later on. He seems to have taken this pretty hard."

"I thought so, too." Horace always seemed to have a great regard for Dolores, and I wondered now if he had been in love with her. I pushed the thought aside, leaving Horace the privacy he deserved. I said, "Not everyone takes comfort in the word of the Lord. By the way, I didn't think of this until now. Did anyone offer a little something to the priest?"

"It's taken care of," said Dunbar.

"And the carriage? I imagine we'll have to settle some accounts when the sister gets here."

Dunbar said, "The stable man wouldn't accept anything for the carriage. And of course Horace insisted on hosting the dinner. So it's just Ted's fee for the burial, and I'm sure we can settle that with no trouble."

"Well," I said, "for one who doesn't go in much for funerals, you've kept track of things better than I have. Then again, I've had very little to do with them, myself."

"The business part is not so hard, especially from the outside. But if you're on the inside, like Emilia or even Horace—well, that can be difficult."

I reflected for a second. "And the sister, too. No telling how she'll take it. What's her name, by the way?"

"Regina. Regina Palomar."

"Palomar. Of course. That was Dolores's last name when she was the governess."

Night had fallen when Dunbar and I set out, and the main street was dark except in a couple of places. I turned up my coat collar against the chill and kept my hands in my pockets. As we crossed the street diagonally at the first corner, I said, "It doesn't look as if there's a light on in the café."

No lights showed in any of the buildings on that side, including the café when we got to it. We peered in through the window, and the interior was dark all the way back.

"Shall we try the saloon?" I said. Halfway down the next block, on the same side of the street, a glow of light fell on the sidewalk and beyond, where a couple of horses stood at the hitching rail.

No one went in or came out as we walked from darkness to soft light. Through the window I saw half a dozen men, but I didn't stop to identify anyone. I took my hands out of my pockets, pushed the door open, and stepped inside with Dunbar behind me.

Horace was standing at the bar, half-turned. He was wearing his Scotch cap and a coarse wool jacket, and he had a drink in front of him. He raised a hand in greeting.

We walked over to join him. I said, "We dropped by to see you, but your place was closed."

"Not much doin'," he said. He raised his eyes to meet mine. "I thought I'd have a drink to cap off a sad day."

"We'll join you, if you don't mind."

"Not at all." Horace signaled to Jim Sloane, who poured two glasses of whiskey. Horace handed us the drinks, raised his, and said, "Here's to the best."

I appreciated his observance of form in not mentioning a woman's name in a saloon. I raised my glass and touched the other two. As I lowered my drink after taking a sip, I became aware of a couple of men down the bar. One seemed to be slouching against a post when no post was present, and the other was standing up straight with his head lifted. Though I did not care for Lee Porter, I had more or less neutral feelings toward him. But a genuine dislike rose within me at the sight of Man Mountain Montgomery. I despised him, I believe, for the arrogant brute that he was, but also because he had come to town not long before Dolores had died. I told myself that two things happening in sequence did not mean that one caused the other, and I reminded myself that two other people had died before Montgomery had come to town. Still, I despised him, and I looked away.

As if they had read me like a book, the two of them sauntered over a minute later. Lee Porter spoke first.

"What brings you boys out on the town?" He raised a cigarette to his lips, and the end of it glowed as he took a drag. He squinted against the rising wisp of smoke.

"It's Saturday night," said Dunbar.

Porter blew smoke out of the side of his mouth. "I thought you had your own private boys' club."

"Not so much," Dunbar replied. "We've been here before, including one of the last times Tim Sexton was seen alive."

"Was he a friend of yours?"

"I didn't know him."

"I didn't think he was, not any more than that young fella you found out at the Frenchman's Quarry."

Dunbar's eyes narrowed, and he kept his silence.

Porter went on. "Dead men seem to follow you around, or vice versa. Or maybe I should say dead people."

"There have been a few to find. But I think you'd have a hard time making a case that I had a hand in any of them."

Porter shrugged in his loose way, and his eyelids drooped a little. His hand wavered as he tapped his ashes on the floor. Between his gestures and his forwardness, I thought he might have had a few drinks already. He said, "You don't seem to care whose property you trespass on, and everyone knows you've got designs on the Frenchman's Quarry."

Dunbar remained calm. "Even if that was true, what would it have to do with the death of Tim Sexton?"

Porter shrugged again, and his lip lifted on one side. "You tell me."

"You seem to be the one who has plenty to say."

"I've already said it, but I can say it clearer. We didn't have any trouble around here until you came to town."

"You sing the same tune as your boss. Only tune you know. You ought to be his deputy. Maybe you are. As for whether there was any trouble before I came, there are people still alive who have a better memory than that."

Porter squinted as he took a last drag on his cigarette. "You know, it would be better if you moved on while it's still easy. Just leave town. No one'll miss you."

"Not till I'm done."

Porter's eyes were still drawn in, and he seemed to be forming another comment. He looked down as he dropped his cigarette butt on the floor and stepped on it. He took a breath as if he was going to speak, but Montgomery interrupted.

"Sure, and there's work to be done." He turned to me, and his stained teeth showed as he said, "Just ask little buddy here."

My blood came right up, and I said, "What do you know about anyone's work?"

A smile spread across his broad face. "I don't have to know much. 'Specially about someone who wears an apron."

"It so happens I don't wear one."

"I'm referrin' to one you might like to lift up. The Mexican girl's."

I lost my judgment. I threw the rest of my drink in his face and said, "Why, you pig!"

He came right back with his meaty right fist and knocked me on my rear end with one punch. I saw floating spots and heard a ringing, tweeting sound. Horace helped me up and handed me my hat as Dunbar stood watching Montgomery.

The man mountain laughed. "Legs a little wobbly? Heh-heh. Well, I was gonna mention somethin' else before you threw your drink at me. You wanna think twice before you knock her up. Eedi-ots run in the family."

Dunbar stepped between us. "I think that's enough. You got your satisfaction. Leave it at that."

"I'm just gettin' started."

"No, you aren't. We don't need any more of your talk."

Montgomery wagged his head. "You mean about the maid? Aw, hell, she's just a—" His right fist came out of nowhere, but Dunbar blocked it.

Jim Sloane's voice came up from behind the bar. "Take it outside, men."

Montgomery gave a broad smile. "Sure. I'll be glad to." He walked to the door with Porter following.

Dunbar took off his hat and coat and handed them to Horace. "Stay back a few steps," he said. "He might be waiting right outside, and you don't want to get in the way." He went to the door, stepped aside as he opened it, and walked out.

When Horace and I got to the door, Dunbar and Montgomery were squaring off in the dim light of the street.

If I hadn't seen Montgomery punch twice already, I would have expected him to be a slow, lumbering fighter. But he wasn't. For all of his bulk, he moved light on his feet as he circled to his left and darted in and out with feints. On one of his maneuvers, Dunbar caught him with a right hook, and he sagged back to stand flat-footed. Dunbar moved in and rocked his head with two more punches.

Montgomery had the deep-seated drive of a fighter, punching back even when he was getting pummeled. The two men separated. Montgomery was seething now, no longer smiling and taunting. He moved forward, setting his foot each time and leaning his weight into each punch. Dunbar took a couple of glancing hits as he backed up, and then he delivered a jab that Montgomery stepped right into. Dunbar hit him two more times. The man mountain backed up, wrinkled his nose, and showed his teeth as he pulled in a breath. Then he shut his mouth and rushed.

Dunbar hit him on the side of the head, pushed his head down, and hit him again. The big man stumbled, caught his footing, and rushed with his head lowered. Instead of punching, he was reaching out and grabbing, first at Dunbar's waist and then at his leg. Dunbar sprawled, and the man moved up for an arm lock around the waist. He moved in and tried to hook his leg around his opponent's. Dunbar pushed the man's head to the side, sprawled again, and came up with Montgomery's leg in his hands. He stepped back, and the man mountain rose up, then leaned to keep his balance as he hopped on his left leg.

Dunbar had him by the calf and the ankle. For a second the two of them were suspended, and Dunbar seemed to have complete mastery of the brute. With one motion he pulled and turned the leg, and the heavy man's other foot left the ground. Everything went out from under him, and he landed on his left arm.

Montgomery rolled over and sat up, holding his left elbow with his other hand.

Dunbar stood back and said, "I'm ready if you want more.

It's up to you."

Pain showed on the thick man's face. "I think I might have broke somethin'. We'll have to finish this some other time."

"Like I say, it's up to you." Dunbar took his hat and coat from Horace. He put on the hat and draped the coat over his arm. He was taking deep breaths, and I imagined he was plenty warm. He said, "Shall we go back in and finish our drinks?"

The next few days were uneventful. Horace told us that Lee Porter had taken Montgomery to Lusk to see a doctor and that the marshal, with his foreman gone, was looking after his ranch and could be found there if something came up.

During this time, Lalo came around more than usual. He said Emilia was staying home and made him go out to get exercise. I imagined he was getting on her nerves, just as he did on mine, making all of his small talk and pestering me to let him ride Pedro.

At last I gave in. I put Pedro's halter on him and wrapped a rope from one side to the other in the form of a continuous rein. I did not have a riding saddle small enough for a donkey, and my regular saddle was at the livery stable, so Lalo climbed on and rode bareback. Pedro trotted up and down the alley, his body bobbing and his hard little hooves taking sure steps. I was afraid Lalo was going to fall off and injure his own arm, but he clamped his legs against the donkey's ribs and grabbed his ruff of a mane when he needed to.

"See?" said Lalo. "He loves me very much, and he lets me ride him. You can give him to me."

"No, Lalo. I need him. But you can ride him. Just remember, you always have to ask permission."

Lalo slid off and put his arms around Pedro's neck. "See how he loves me?"

"Of course he does. That's why he lets you ride him. If he

didn't like you, he would throw you in the dirt."

Lalo rubbed the animal's soft nose. With his characteristic jump in logic he said, "And when does the sister of Doña Dolores arrive?"

"Tomorrow, Lalo. Tomorrow is Wednesday."

"My sister is very sad since the death of the lady."

"Yes, and with reason. Let us hope that everything goes well with the sister."

Regina Palomar arrived in the same carriage Dunbar had used to fetch the priest for Doña Dolores's funeral. I had gone to Dolores's house to be on hand when Emilia received the lady, and Lalo let us know when the carriage arrived at the edge of town. So Emilia and I were on the doorstep when Dunbar wheeled the buggy around and brought it to a stop. He set the brake, climbed down, and came around to give her a hand.

She was wearing a dark brown wool cloak with a hood, so I didn't see much of her at first. She seemed agile enough, however, as she stepped down from the carriage, and her dark brown eyes were quick and bright.

Dunbar introduced us around, and Emilia walked Regina to the house, holding her by both hands and expressing her condolences in Spanish. Dunbar lifted two leather valises out of the vehicle, and we each carried one into the house. Emilia had seats for us all in the front room.

I directed my attention to Regina and said, "I hope you had a good trip. I'm sure it was a long one."

"Oh, yes. Quite long." She had laid back the hood and taken off the cloak when she sat down, so her features were visible now. She had dark hair, wrapped and gathered in back, and her complexion was clear. Her face was firm, and her figure was well kept. She looked ten years younger than her sister, though I doubted the difference was that great, as Dolores had aged forward and this woman had held the line quite well.

"Do you find it cold here?" asked Dunbar.

She smiled at him. "I have seen snow in Santa Fe, I assure you, but the weather was still warm when I left. So, yes, it is a little colder here, but I came prepared."

Emilia spoke in English. "Are you hungry after your long trip? You are at home in your sister's house, and I am at your service. My brother and I will stay here, so you will not be alone. So please be at home, with confidence."

Regina answered, speaking to all of us. "I am not very hungry right now, but, yes, I would like to have something in a while. I would like to invite these two gentlemen to join us. Say, at five o'clock? That will give me time to get settled in."

Dunbar stood up, hat in hand, and I did the same. He said, "That will give me time to put the carriage away." He nodded to me.

I turned to Regina and said, "I imagine you would like to go to the cemetery before long."

She smiled as before. "I have already been there. Mr. Dunbar took me by on our way from the train station. But thank you for thinking of me. And I am sure I will want to go again."

"Very well," I said. "Until five."

Emilia had cut up and cooked two chickens in a gravy. She set the large clay dish on a board on the table, next to a dish of boiled potatoes. As Emilia began to serve the plates, Regina frowned.

"I would like you to sit with us," she said. "And your brother, too, if he would like. We have a great many things to talk about."

"Lalo prefers to eat in the kitchen," Emilia said, still in English. "And I can tend to him there. We will eat after the rest of you do."

"Very well. Then you'll be here as we eat?"

"Oh, yes. To serve you." Emilia picked up the plate she had set down.

Regina looked across the table at Dunbar and me. "I am sure we have things to talk about. But we are in no hurry. Please enjoy your meal."

Dunbar glowed as he said, "With the honor of your presence, we could not do otherwise."

She gave him a modest smile in return. "Did you study oratory, or French literature?"

He laughed. "Neither. I didn't make it that far. I'm sorry if I got carried away by the moment."

She smiled again. "You did all right. At least you didn't lapse into *'Belle marquise, vos beaux yeux me font mourir d'amour.'*"

"I don't know that one."

"It's from an old comedy. By Molière." She turned to me. "And you, Mr. Gregor? You haven't said much."

"I don't know much. But at your encouragement, I fully intend to enjoy my meal."

"How very nice." She waited until Emilia served the three plates, and then with a serious tone she said, "This is an amiable gathering, and I feel comfortable in your presence, but the occasion for my being here is all very unexpected. I had not seen my sister for years, but she wrote me every month or so, and I had no indication that she had any danger to her health."

I said, "I don't believe any of us did. She seemed in nothing less than good health. Sad, perhaps, from the troubles she had seen, but not fragile or on the verge of anything."

"I'll put it more plainly," said Dunbar. "I don't believe the marshal and the coroner's conclusion that she died of natural causes."

"Nor do I," said Regina. "From the time that the little boy died, I've had the feeling that things were not right in this town. I did not think that things were right with my sister, either, but

I did not know in what way. Then when she died without warning—well, I have to be skeptical. I just didn't know if anyone here would be willing to speak up about it."

I found it encouraging that she was not intimidated by circumstances in the town. I said, "There are a few of us. I can't speak for anyone else, but for my part, I was hoping you might bring something with you."

"Something like—?"

"Well, if not answers, at least information or some kind of a hint."

She tipped her head. "I can't say that I brought anything of that nature. Whatever there is, it has been here all along."

Dunbar gave her a questioning look. "Really? I would think that if she wrote to you every month or so, she would have dropped a hint at some time or another. Made some mention."

"Well, she didn't, I'm sorry to say. But we'll have a chance to sort through some of her effects, and we might find something."

After dinner, with the help of Emilia, Regina brought out some of her sister's old keepsakes. Among them was a portfolio of drawings she had made and portraits she had painted in the days when she was a governess. There was a pencil drawing of an apple with practiced shading. After that came a bowl of pomegranates, in color. Then came a series of small paintings—a ring of keys, a cat, a mutton-chop terrier, a vase of roses. My heart began to beat stronger as I saw colored portraits of blond-haired, blue-eyed Angélique; little André, with his mother's hair and eyes; and stern Pierre himself, square-headed with wavy dark hair, dark side whiskers, flushed cheeks, and blue eyes. All of the portraits, like the still lifes before them, were signed "D.P."

"Not a picture of herself from those younger days," I said. "Though as I recall, she looked quite a bit as you do now."

"She was much prettier—and younger, too, of course."

Dunbar did not play in with gallantry at this point. He said, "One would hope that among these things there would be a diary or a journal or something like that."

Regina shook her head. "Not in these things."

"That's too bad," I said. "And of all the letters she wrote to you—"

"I'll tell you this." Regina looked at each of us and then at Emilia. "This can go no further than the four of us for right now. But she wrote me one thing, which I received just a day before I heard from you. She said that in the event of her unexpected death, I could find in her safe-deposit box a letter, which was to be read in the presence of at least three people."

"That's big," said Dunbar.

"Yes, it is, and it is partly the reason I am skeptical about the coroner's report."

"He's not much of a coroner," I said. "He's just the barber, and he works in conjunction with the marshal."

Dunbar spoke again. "If it's a safe-deposit box, we'll need a key."

Regina gave a self-assured smile. "Don't worry about that. Dolores kept a key, and she mailed one to me."

Dunbar said, "Let us imagine that someone might have had the opportunity to look through her things. Might they, in the absence of a document, have found the key?"

Regina smiled. "It was inside Our Lady of Sorrows." She nodded toward a plaster-of-Paris figurine of a pious-looking woman, her hands clasped and her head bent, dressed in a blue hooded cloak with a white shawl enclosing her face. "Dolores painted that, by the way. But the key's not there now. I have the two of them in safe, separate places."

I felt as if I had been holding my breath. Now I knew what she meant when she said everything had been here all along. I breathed out and said, "She didn't indicate which three people should be present for the reading, did she?"

"No, just a minimum of three. But I'm sure we'd like to have someone outside our own circle."

"I can think of a couple," I said. In reality, I could think of more people than had come to Dolores's funeral who would like to hear the contents, and I wasn't sure we would want to invite them all.

CHAPTER TEN

Dunbar and I took leave of the women and stepped out into the chilly evening. I turned up my collar and put on my gloves as we walked away from the house. Dunbar had put on his gloves as we stood inside saying good night, and now he was flexing his hands as we got under way on our walk back to the lodging house. I was reflecting on a couple of different moments when it seemed as if Regina had noticed the mark in the palm of his hand. It seemed as if she trusted both of us, but I wouldn't have blamed her if she had retained some skepticism or had held back some bit of confidential information.

My thoughts ran on like that as we walked in the quiet evening. We had turned right and crossed the street at the first corner, and we had almost reached the main street when a ghastly sound pierced the air. I almost jumped out of my tracks as I flinched and turned. Dunbar stopped short and turned as well.

The noise came again, and I thought it might be Lalo. It sounded like his howl, though it was louder and fuller. Dunbar and I together set off at a run in the direction of the house we had just left.

The howl sounded again and again, at intervals of about twenty seconds. We reached the house, where the noise was coming from the east side. We followed the sound, and there in the shadows of night, Lalo was struggling with another person. His call rang out in the night air. *Ah-woo-oo!*

Closer, I saw that Lalo had his arms locked around a man who was thrashing and elbowing and trying to get free. The man was of average size and not wearing a hat.

We came to a stop, and Dunbar said in a commanding tone, "Whoa! What's this?"

The man threw another elbow and said, "Dammit!" Then he stood still, and though his voice was not as calm as if he was leaning against a post, I recognized it as Lee Porter's. "I caught this fool prowling around," he said.

"Beeg liar!" said Lalo. He gave Porter a squeeze and a shake.

Dunbar said, "Let him go."

Lalo released his grip, and Porter turned away. As he did, he swung around and hit Lalo on the side of the head.

Dunbar stepped forward and landed a punch on Porter's jaw.

The man staggered back, stood up, and said, "What the hell?"

"Keep your hand away from your gun," said Dunbar, "and we'll get to the bottom of this."

Lalo let out a stream in Spanish. "He was hiding, snooping. I found him, and I grabbed him."

Porter said, "Tell him to talk English."

"He's talking to me, and I understand him just fine," said Dunbar. "He says he came upon you where you were snooping."

"What a lie."

"Save your breath," Dunbar said. "Like I said, we'll get to the bottom of it."

A voice from behind us said, "I'll say we will."

I turned and made out the form of Pat Roderick. He stood against a glow of light that came out of the front of the house.

From behind him, a female's voice, Regina's, said, "What is it?"

"We've got a prowler," said Dunbar.

Lee Porter spoke up. "I found this half-wit here, and now he claims he found me."

"Well, we'll take him in," said the marshal.

Dunbar's voice was unwavering as he said, "Wait a minute. We've got two men here. Each one says the other was prowling, but Lalo was the one who had this fellow under control."

"I'll believe my foreman over the village idiot."

"Not so fast," said Dunbar. "If you take anyone in, you'd better take 'em both."

Roderick said, "And on whose authority are you telling me that?"

"I can't say that I've got authority, but I'll tell you this. On the day she died, earlier that day, Dolores told me, in the presence of two other people, that someone had been lurking around her house. You can bet it wasn't Lalo, and you can bet that's why he was on the lookout. Even if your foreman, as you call him, did come upon someone else, let's ask him what he was doing in this neighborhood at this hour to begin with. Not looking after cows, I'll warrant that."

Neither Roderick nor Porter said a word.

Regina came forward, drawing her cloak about her. Emilia followed with a lamp held up. As I got a better look, I saw that another man had appeared in the background as well.

He was dressed for colder weather, as he wore a fur cap and a wool overcoat. The lamplight showed on his face, and I recognized the heavy-lidded eyes of Ross Ferguson.

"What's the big problem?" he said. "I could hear this all the way from my house."

Roderick raised his head and squared his shoulders. "Someone's been prowling."

"I gathered that. What I meant was, if this man of yours was doing something, why don't you take him in?"

"I don't know that he was."

"Oh, come on, now. This other one had him collared. Right's

right, and fair's fair. If you're going to take anyone in, it should be him."

Roderick's voice came out sharp. "I'm going to take 'em both in, is what I'm goin' to do. If people would just let me do my job." He turned to Lalo and Porter. "Did both of you get that? Are you goin' to go without any trouble?"

"Fine with me," said Porter, who had relaxed into a slouch. "You'll find out soon enough I wasn't doin' anything."

Roderick half-turned and spoke in a loud, deliberate voice. "How about you? You understand what I said, don't you?"

"I go," said Lalo.

"Well, you can both spend the night in the pokey, and we'll get this straightened out tomorrow." Roderick shook his head. "Sometimes I wonder how ridiculous things can get."

Dunbar said, "Don't make too light of it. A woman died in this house."

"Well, I'm sorry," Roderick snapped. "But people die every day. Right now, all across this country there are people—"

Regina's voice cut in. "I beg you, too, not to make light of this matter."

Roderick seemed to see her for the first time. His eyes studied her, and I wondered if he was comparing her to her sister or if he was trying to determine how much trouble she could cause him.

"I'm sorry," he said. "I let this man get under my skin. You must be Mrs. Carreau's sister." At her nod, he continued. "I'm sorry for the loss of your sister. It was a great shock to all of us. She had been here for a long time and had seen a lot of sad things."

Regina's voice was firm as she said, "She was not that old."

"Of course not. She had a lot to live for. All the same, she lived longer than the rest of the Carreau family."

The tone of Roderick's voice gave me the impression that he

was trying to advance his own point.

Regina, still calm, replied, "I realized that when I saw their gravestones. But enough of this subject. I won't keep you from your work."

"Not at all." Roderick put his thumbs in his gunbelt and turned away from Regina. "Are you two ready to go?"

"Any time," said Porter.

Dunbar sniffed. "We can go along with you. Mr. Gregor and I were on our way home when this commotion started." He nodded in recognition to Ross Ferguson and said to the marshal and me, "I'll see the ladies to the door and be right with you."

Ferguson said, "I'll go home, then."

We made a strange company, I thought as we walked along, but the marshal seemed untroubled. Dunbar and I left him at the jail with his two prisoners, and we continued on our way to the lodging house.

It was cold inside. I lit a lamp and did not take off my coat. I said, "I think I might get into the habit of locking the door."

"Not a bad idea." Dunbar flexed his hands but did not take off his gloves. "By the way, no need to get too comfortable. I told the ladies we'd be back in a little bit. They'll let us in the back door."

"You don't think there'll be any more trouble tonight, do you?"

"You can never tell. But it'll give the women peace of mind."

We went out the back door and into the night again. We navigated wide of the town by about a quarter of a mile and came around to the back door of Dolores's house. Everything was quiet as before, and with only a light tap we were let in.

Once inside, we stayed away from the windows so that we wouldn't cast shadows on the curtains. Dunbar asked Emilia to set the lamps closer to the windows of the house so that any shadows would be cast inward. After some discussion, we agreed

159

that Dunbar and I would spend the night in the spare room. Emilia said she would sleep in Dolores's room with Regina.

The night was still young, not yet eight o'clock. Regina said she would like to spend some more time looking through Dolores's papers and other effects. Dunbar had seen a stack of old newspapers in the spare room, so we brought those out to the front room to give us a way to while away the time.

For the next couple of hours, he and I browsed through the papers. I read old accounts of water projects, railroad construction, weather conditions, wheat production, cattle prices, and the sundry mishaps and misdoings of people. I found it interesting to see how many of these items, such as a two-week period of sub-zero weather, only two or three years in the past, now meant nothing. Others, such as the report of a sixteen-year-old girl gone missing, seemed as important as the day they were written.

At a little after ten, Regina came into the sitting room and said she was going to turn in for the night. She went back into Dolores's study and from there into the bedroom. The room we were going to sleep in was in the front corner of the house, on the left side as one went in through the front door. The room the women were going to sleep in was adjacent but with no door connecting. One door led in from the study, and another led in from the back area by the pantry and the water closet. On the right side of the house, off the hallway that led from the front room to the back door, sat the dining room and the kitchen. We had said earlier that we would sleep with our door open to the front room, so Emilia waited until we went in where our two pallets lay on the floor, and then she blew out the lamps.

Darkness settled in as I took off my boots. I said, "I don't expect anything tonight, but as you said, this should give the women some peace of mind."

"I hope so," said Dunbar. "You can tell that Emilia is worried about Lalo, and as for Regina, she seems to have plenty of courage. But this is all new to her, and there are a few good reasons to be afraid." He sniffed. "I'm glad to give a sense of security, but you never know what someone might try to make out of it, what with our sneaking in and then spending the night under the same roof as two unmarried women."

"Honi soit qui mal y pense," I said.

"What's that?"

"An old chivalric motto. It means, 'Shamed be he who thinks ill of it.' "

"That's a good one. I'll try to remember to write it down when the light of day comes around."

I spelled it for him, letter by letter, and said, "I'll spell it for you again tomorrow if you'd like."

"Thanks," he said. "I'll see if I can remember it. Meanwhile, good night."

"The same to you." Earlier in the evening I had wondered how well I would sleep in the room where Dolores had been laid out prior to her burial, but now the morbid thoughts had given way to fancy. I imagined Dunbar as a knight and myself as his squire, while Regina was the lady fair, and Emilia her attendant. We were camped on guard while the ladies slept in a canopied bed in the castle proper. It was a nice set of thoughts to go to sleep by.

I awoke to that kind of silence that hangs in the air after there has been a noise out of place. From Dunbar's breathing I could tell he was sitting up. I raised to my elbows and whispered, "What is it?"

He whispered back, "I'm not sure. I think someone either went out or came in through the back door."

I heard him turn his blankets aside and draw his feet up under him. I had not seen or heard him take off his gunbelt when he crawled into his blankets, and I was listening for the sound of him either loosening his gun in its holster or drawing it, when a woman's scream pierced the air.

The long, sharp scream sounded a second time, accompanied by the shrieks of a second woman, whom I took to be Emilia. I scrambled to my feet as Dunbar, sock-footed, bolted out of the room.

A confusion of sounds rose—Dunbar's footsteps going from one room to the next, furniture bumping and scraping, Emilia calling *"Ayyy!"* and Regina shouting something like "Out! Out!" Footsteps retreated through the back of the house, and then came the abrupt, loud blast of a pistol shot.

I ran down the hallway and reached the open space between the kitchen and the pantry just as Dunbar did.

"It's me," I said.

"I think he went out. The door's open."

"Was that you that fired?"

"Yes, it was. A shot in the dark, as they say. One quick chance, and that was it. Let's get a light." He turned toward the room where the women were. "Ho! Can we get a light?"

"I'll go get one from the front room," I said. By the light of a match, I found one of the lamps. By the time I got it lit and carried it back to the kitchen, Emilia had arrived with another lamp.

She held the lamp at shoulder height, with Regina at her side. Dunbar was bent over, studying the floor.

"It looks like I hit something. This is a drop of blood. Let's see a little further." He stood up partway and moved forward as Emilia did.

I joined the group and added to the light.

Dunbar bent over again. "See the way this drop hit? He was running at this point."

The four of us moved to the door, and the light from our two lamps spilled for a ways into the back yard.

Dunbar stepped outside and stood on the top step. He said, "It'll be hard to follow someone very far in the dark unless he leaves quite a trail. Shh!"

From perhaps half a mile away, well beyond the southern edge of town, came the sound of hoofbeats.

"I don't think we're going to get him tonight." Dunbar put his six-gun in his holster. "We might be able to pick up a trail in the morning."

Regina said, "He came in this way, didn't he? He must have had a key."

Dunbar turned to speak to her. "Skeleton key," he said. "These aren't hard locks to get into for someone who knows how. I don't suppose you got a look at him at all, did you?"

"Not in the least. All I know is that when he put his hand over my mouth, his fingers smelled like nicotine."

"That's something," said Dunbar.

"It's so repugnant, that someone can come into your house like that. Loathsome. Like a snake."

Dunbar said, "I agree. And I don't feel sorry for him if he's got a bullet in him." He stepped back inside and closed the door behind him. "Well, I guess we try to go back to sleep. For what it's worth, we could put a chair against the door as well as lock it."

Regina said, "We'll do that." She raised her head in the lamplight and said, "Thank you. I'm glad you were here."

Grey light had filtered into the house when I awoke. I realized I had heard someone stirring in the kitchen. Dunbar's bed was empty, so I got up and put on my boots. Carrying my coat and hat, I made my way to the kitchen.

Emilia was by herself, slicing potatoes on the sideboard.

Warmth was spreading from the stove, and a coffeepot sat on top.

"Good morning," I said.

"Good morning. Mr. Dunbar went out a little while ago."

"Oh." I was about to put on my hat and coat when I heard someone on the back steps. The door opened, and Dunbar came in.

He said, "I think we've got a trail to follow. We can get our horses as soon as we've had breakfast. Assuming you'd like to go along."

"Of course." I had formed the impression that Dunbar didn't mind having me along as a kind of witness to confirm what happened. Yet I was sure that if at any moment he wanted to do without me, he would do just that.

Emilia set the potatoes to frying and began slicing bacon. "It won't be long," she said.

In a little while, both skillets were crackling, and the aroma of fried potatoes and bacon carried on the air. Emilia poured us each a cup of coffee.

I could tell Dunbar was impatient to get going, so when the food came off the stove, I did not waste time. Dunbar cleaned his plate in good time as well, and we thanked Emilia for the meal.

"*Gracias a Dios,*" she said. Thanks be to God.

The morning was grey and crisp as we walked down the street to the livery stable. No one was out and about, but smoke came from a few stovepipes.

Inside the stable, Dunbar spoke to Jess Fluornoy and began to get the horses ready. As he brushed the blue roan, he tossed out a casual question as to whether the marshal was in town.

"He came for his horse last night and left for his ranch."

"With two men in the calaboose?"

"Well, as he put it, without his foreman, he had to go out to his ranch to tend to his stock."

"He went by himself, then."

"Not that I could verify. He had me saddle a horse for his other hired man. The one who's supposed to do his quarry work."

"I guess he couldn't do the chores himself, huh?"

"Hard to handle a pitchfork with one arm in a sling."

"I suppose that's true," said Dunbar.

He finished saddling the roan and proceeded to brush, comb, and saddle the buckskin. We led the horses out into the morning, which was still grey. A cloud cover had formed in the night, and I wondered if we were going to get some snow.

We mounted up and rode south of town. When we were well beyond the houses, Dunbar spoke.

"What did you think of what the stable man said?"

"About the marshal? It seemed a little odd. How about you?"

"I would bet that if you knew which room to listen in on at the boarding house, you could hear Mr. Montgomery snoring like a bulldog at this very moment."

"Really? How do you figure it?"

"Well, the marshal doesn't smoke, does he?"

"Not that I've ever noticed."

"Nor does Montgomery. From the looks of his teeth I'd say he chews tobacco, but I haven't seen him do that, either."

"So you think the man whose hand smells of nicotine is the foreman of the Rock Canyon Ranch."

"That's my guess. I think he was going to go back to the jail but had the horse ready in case he needed it. That left Man Mountain on foot, so I would guess he hoofed it back to the boarding house."

"Why didn't we go by the jail to see if Porter was there?"

"Because I think we'll find him out here."

"At the ranch?"

"Or somewhere along the way. Depending on how well I hit him."

I gave a low whistle. "You know, it all makes sense, except one thing. If the marshal is behind all of this, which it sure seems he is, I wonder why. What stake does he have in it?"

"That's the part we've got to come up with on our own. You can bet we'll never get it out of him."

"Do you think Porter was after the letter?"

"Some kind of evidence, I would say. Just as it occurred to you, someone might think Regina brought something with her. Then again, we don't know if it was Porter. . . . If we find someone else out here leaking blood, like Ted the barber—or, even less likely, Horace—we've got to start over. By the way, wouldn't it have been nice if Regina had come to breakfast?"

"Do you think there's something in that as well?"

"Oh, no. I just thought she would have added something to the atmosphere. Not that I minded your company, of course, but she *is*—"

"No doubt. She has a very nice presence." I wondered how he could be so jovial when we were looking for a wounded fugitive. I said, "Back to the main subject. What if this fellow we're looking for is in really bad shape, or even dead?"

"I don't feel a bit sorry for someone like that, whoever it is. I just hope it's someone we didn't care for to begin with."

"You think there's a chance it might not be?"

"There's always a chance. As you go through life, you learn of this person or that, you even know one sometimes, and it turns out he did something hideous. People say, 'Oh, he wouldn't do something like that.' But you never know someone a hundred percent."

"You think it could be someone like Horace, then?"

"Not very likely. But to be on the safe side, don't rule it out until you know for sure. If you want an assumption to live by, it's that everyone is at least capable of doing something dark or terrible."

"Even Emilia?"

He shrugged. "We're on the theoretical level. Let's look sharp now, because this is where we ought to be able to pick up the trail."

I poked along as he rode in irregular, overlapping circles. After a few minutes he came to a stop and said, "Here it is, I think." He swung down and knelt, then raised his head and looked to the west.

He mounted up and rode on, traveling in an S-shaped pattern. I rode along a few yards to the right. The sun was not breaking through the cloud cover, and there seemed to be humidity in the air, as the horse hooves fell soft on the short, dry grass. When Dunbar's course straightened out, I could see we were headed toward the Rock Canyon Ranch and Bluestone Quarry.

Our way led west and kept to the south of the main trail from town to the ranch. A little over half an hour into the ride, I saw the old railroad bed to my left, where it angled in from the east toward the quarry. Ahead and to my right, the land sloped up to a low hill that blocked the ranch house from view.

I rode alongside Dunbar and said, "Headed for the quarry."

"Looks like it."

I imagined Lee Porter holed up in the rocks like one of the rattlesnakes he talked about. I nudged the buckskin and gave Dunbar a wide berth again to follow the signs.

Our trail met up with the old railroad bed, and we rode along the flank of it. It passed through a low spot between a hill and a larger hill. In another minute the view opened up, and we were riding into the canyon at the entrance to the city of stones. As before, I saw piles of rock and upright formations. The scene was duller than on our earlier visit, as the sky was still overcast, and the paths between the rocks lay in dimmer light. As we brought our horses to a stop, the world went quiet. The air was still, without a breath of wind stirring. I recalled the word that had come to me in this place almost two weeks earlier. *Necropolis.* City of the dead.

A small clicking sound broke the silence. Dunbar's face tensed as he turned an ear. The sound came again. Dunbar eased himself down from the saddle with a faint creak of leather and a brush of cloth. I did the same. The sound carried again, a little different this time, less abrupt. I thought I recognized it as the uneven movement of animal hooves. I glanced at Dunbar, who was intent on listening. I motioned for him to give me his reins, and then I flinched at the sound of a horse's whinny.

Dunbar had his gun drawn as he handed me his reins. With his back to a mass of rock, he edged around. Beyond the rock, a horse snuffled. Dunbar moved around, out of sight for a minute, then came back and waved for me.

I went forward, leading the two horses. Dunbar's tall, black hat moved as he motioned with his head. I came up beside him and saw an object out of place among the dull stones.

The body of a man was sitting up, slumped a little to the side. His dust-colored hat was tipped forward, cockeyed, and his right hand held a six-gun in his lap. If it had not been for the dark stain on his light brown vest, it might have seemed as if Lee Porter had gotten tired of standing and leaning against a rock column and had found a place to sit.

The horse snuffled from fifty feet away. It was a sorrel ranch horse with its reins trailing on the crumbly rock floor. I thought it was the same horse I had seen in this place the last time.

I turned to Dunbar and said, "As you thought."

"Not a big surprise." With his gun still drawn, Dunbar walked forward and stood in front of Porter's body. With the toe of his boot he pushed against Porter's upright boot. "Gettin' kind of stiff. I doubt that his boss knows he's here."

We led our horses out the way we came, then mounted up. We rode through the mouth of the canyon and into the flat area where the unfinished stone house stood in silence like the ruins of an old church. I could not see where anyone had made any progress on it. When we rode past it I looked back, and as on that earlier occasion, it seemed to be standing at the gateway to the city of stones and the city of the dead.

I said to Dunbar, not very loud, "What do you think of the story he told us that day about the pit?"

"Typical story, I guess. Maybe a little bit of the bogeyman. Why?"

"I wondered if he just wanted to keep us out of there. Like they had something they didn't want anyone to find."

"Like someone buried?"

"Either that, or the secret canyon through the rock."

Dunbar gave a light shrug. "Could be they just don't want people to know any more than necessary. On the other hand, to follow my own philosophy, I suppose we should never rule out another body. In the present case, as far as dead people go, everyone is accounted for. How and why some of them died, now that's the part that has yet to be accounted for."

CHAPTER ELEVEN

Smoke was rising from the stovepipe of the ranch house as we rode into the yard. The horse hooves made hollow sounds as they struck the hard, bare ground, and I was not surprised to see the door move inward. Marshal Roderick appeared in the doorway. He had his star pinned to his leather vest, and his gun hung at his hip. He was wearing a neat-fitting grey wool shirt, wool pants, spurred boots, and his hat. His brown eyes moved back and forth as he looked us over.

"What do you want?" he asked.

Dunbar swung down from his horse and took a couple of steps forward. "Thought we'd save you some time."

"Is that right? Next thing I know, you'll be claimin' to be doin' me a favor."

"I won't go that far."

"Well, say what you came for. I need to get back to work."

"I'm sure you're anxious to get back, so I'm glad we caught you when we did."

I slid down from my horse. The marshal gave me a contemptuous look, then turned to Dunbar and said, "If you're gonna save me time, just spit it out."

"I don't know if you know where to find your man Lee Porter, but you can start back in the quarry there." Dunbar motioned with the thumb of his gloved hand.

Roderick's eyes narrowed. "What's he doing there?"

"Nothing at all. He's stone cold dead."

The marshal's face hardened, and his jaw moved sideways. "I don't think you're very funny."

"I don't mean to be. There's nothing funny about this."

"Then how does it come to be that he's in the quarry and you know about it?"

"It's an interesting series of events, but before I tell you, I'd like to ask where your other hired man, Montgomery, is at the moment."

A queasy expression passed over Roderick's face. "What's that got to do with anything?"

Dunbar shrugged. "Well, it was said that he left the livery stable with you."

Roderick's eyes wavered. "His arm was hurting too much, so he turned around and went back."

"He must have forgotten to turn the horse in. It was that sorrel that Lee Porter usually rode, wasn't it?"

The muscles on the marshal's face shifted as he clenched his teeth. He seemed to be weighing his chances. "Yeh," he said. "That was the one."

Good gamble, I thought.

Dunbar said, "Well, if you weren't there, you might not know how it happened. But that horse fell back into the hands of Lee Porter."

"Lee's in jail. You saw to that."

"I saw that he got put there. But somewhere along midnight, he found a way to creep inside a house where he didn't belong, and someone shot him for an intruder. In the morning we tracked him out this way, and that's how we came to find him in the quarry."

"I don't believe it."

"Go see for yourself. And when you do, you'll see he's been there for a few hours."

The marshal's chest moved up and down as he took a breath.

171

He said, "Look here. Lee's my foreman, and he wouldn't do something that wasn't on the square. He's got his pride. I knew he was offended at being arrested, but he went along."

"Sure he did," said Dunbar. "We all saw it."

"So I don't know what you're trying to pull with what you're saying now."

"Nothing. But he's not in jail. You're going to have to find him, and I'm telling you where you can do it."

"I don't believe it."

"Don't take my word for it. Go see for yourself." Dunbar turned away, gave me a toss of the head, and led his horse out to mount up.

As I turned to follow, the marshal spoke.

"Don't come back."

Dunbar swung into the saddle with one hand on the horn. He looked down at the marshal and said, "I'm not done."

As I followed him out of the ranch yard, I did not look back. I had the dread feeling that things were falling apart and that when the pretending was over, something bad was going to happen.

Half a mile later, I rode alongside Dunbar and said, "Things are going to have to be out in the open before long."

"You'd think so," he said, "but some people can fight the truth for a long time after it's plain that there's no way they can beat it."

Back in town, we put away the horses at the livery stable and walked the three blocks to Doña Dolores's house. Emilia let us in, and Regina invited us to sit down in the front room. We took off our hats and sat in the two chairs with red upholstery.

Dunbar told her, without ceremony, that we had followed the trail and had found the body of the man who had been caught lurking around the house the evening before.

Regina said, "It's too bad he had to die that way, but spying on someone's house is bad enough. Entering another person's house in the middle of the night is far worse."

Dunbar stared at his hat, which he had sitting on his knee. He said, "We'll see what comes of it." After a pause he said, "How are things here?"

Regina shrugged. "As good as can be expected. I've had time to think about things, and I wonder if someone was eavesdropping and heard me mention the letter that's in safe keeping."

Dunbar raised his eyebrows. "It occurred to me as well. But it is also possible that no one heard anything in particular but thought you might have brought some evidence with you."

"It could be." Regina paused. "I'm rather apprehensive about this whole matter, to say the least. But I feel it's my duty to follow through and read that letter."

Dunbar nodded.

"I think tomorrow would be neither too soon nor too late." She let her eyes rest on me.

"I agree," I said.

Regina continued. "In the meanwhile, I'd like to visit the bank and assure myself that the letter is there. I think I might do it under cover of taking something more for safe keeping."

I said, "If you're thinking of going there in the next while, we can go with you."

"It's kind of you to offer. I would appreciate it. After all, I don't know this town or anyone else in it."

"It's our pleasure to keep you company," said Dunbar. "At your convenience."

"Well, there's no need for me to keep you waiting. I can be ready in a few minutes, and then we can go."

A cool breeze met us from the northwest as we stepped out of the house, and the sky was still overcast. Regina was wearing her dark wool cloak with the loose sleeves, but she did not put up her hood. She held her head up so that the breeze played on her features and caused her to hold her face in a half-smile. Her dark hair moved, and from my side I saw a round, turquoise earring set in silver. Also on the breeze I caught a dry trace of aroma that I thought must have come from a powder she had put on. That in itself would have disposed me to like her if I didn't already.

When we reached the main street, we crossed to the north side, where the breeze was lighter in the lee of the buildings. We walked past the mercantile and the general store, where Ben the clerk was standing inside in the center aisle, hands on his hips, looking out at us. I waved to him, then peered inside the larger window as we walked past. Ross Ferguson sat at this desk farther in, half-turned away from us, holding up a sheet of paper to read by the incoming light.

A block later, we came to the bank. Henry Lauck, the clerk, put on an automatic smile as he stood at his window with his hands folded together on the counter.

"Good morning," he said. "How can I help you?"

Being the town resident of our group, I took the lead. "Good morning. As you may know, this lady is Miss Regina Palomar. She is Dolores Carreau's sister, and she has come to town to look after some of her sister's interests."

Henry's smile returned. "We'll be happy to assist in any way we can. I'm Henry Lauck. Pleased to meet you." He nodded his head.

"Likewise," said Regina. She drew an oilskin envelope out of the pocket of her cloak and set it on the counter. "One of the things my sister told me about was a safe-deposit box. I would like to put something in it."

"Oh, yes. You have a key, I imagine?"

"Yes, I do." Regina's face broke into a warm smile.

Henry might have been a few years younger than Regina, but

the distance was not so great that he could resist. His face relaxed, and his eyes opened. In a more lively tone than before, he said, "Very well. I'll get the key to the vault, and I'll show you the way."

He went to an inner office by the street window, and I heard Walter Eliot's commanding voice. In a few seconds, Henry came out. He was wearing what I took to be a gallant smile. He said, "This way," and walked in brisk steps along his side of the counter to the center of the bank.

Regina walked along on her side, still smiling. At the end of the counter she joined him and walked with him to the iron gate. The keys jingled, the lock clicked, and the metal clanged. Henry opened the gate, and Regina's voice had a cheerful tone as she thanked him. The two of them went into the narrow passageway and out of my sight, and then Henry reappeared. He stood and lingered at the gate, wearing a bland expression. From my parents' time I knew that the safe-deposit boxes each had a separate lock and were mounted in a wall on the left. On the right side of that dim passage, a heavy door with a combination and a lever handle led into the vault proper where the money was kept.

I heard the sounds of the little door being opened and the box being slid out. Meanwhile, Henry was restless as he stood by the gate. I imagined he was following his boss's instructions as he craned his neck every two or three seconds to see what she was doing. At one point, he gave an embarrassed smile and a tiny laugh, but within a few seconds he was peeking again.

The metallic sounds came in reverse order as the box was put away and the door was closed. Footsteps brought Regina back to the gate, where she had another pleasant exchange of words with the clerk. Henry closed the gate behind her with a muffled clang, turned the key in the lock, and gave Regina a slight bow of the head. As they walked back to the front part of the bank, the counter separated them.

"Thank you so very much," she said. "I'll see you tomorrow, then. At about nine."

"Entirely my pleasure," Henry answered.

The door opened from the inner office behind him, and Walter Eliot appeared. He was a tall man, bald-headed and clean-shaven, with dark, greying hair and round spectacles. He wore a dark suit and vest that showed the spread of middle age. Raising his hand to his necktie as if to straighten it, he said, "Is everything in order?"

"Yes, sir," said Henry. His enlivened tone vanished. "This is Miss Palomar. And this is Mr. Dunbar, who lodges with Mr. Gregor."

Eliot's eyes took in Regina, skimmed over me, flickered at Dunbar, and came back to rest on Regina. "Pleased to meet you," he said. "If you need anything, we're at your service."

"Thank you," she said. "Mr. Lauck has been most courteous."

I thought she had worked her own charm quite well. "Very good," said Eliot. His eyes went to his clerk. "When you have a minute, Henry." As he turned to go back into his office, I saw that he had a ruler in his left hand. I imagined he was going to resume reading a ledger, and I was sure he had a magnifying glass close at hand as well.

The cast-iron skillet had a glossy black shine to it, and thin black smoke was beginning to rise. I took it off the stove and set it on a board to cool. I had swabbed it with bacon grease after I cleaned it, and now everything was tidied up after the midday meal and dishes.

A knock at the front door startled me. I wondered who it might be. Dunbar had gone to his room, to his brown study, while I cleaned up the kitchen. I had taken to locking the front door but not in the daytime, so even if he had gone out, he would have done no more than a routine knock as he let himself in.

I opened the door, and there stood Lalo. He had a small cloth bundle in his hands.

I spoke to him in Spanish as usual. "Good afternoon, Lalo. What a surprise to see you. When did they let you out?"

"A little before dinner time. He was very grouchy, the man with the star."

"I didn't know he was in town. He didn't tell you anything, did he?"

"No, but my sister did. She said the foreman came around again in the middle of the night, and Mr. Dunbar gave it to him with a bullet."

"Something like that. But tell me, what do you have there?"

Lalo smiled. "Something for Pedro." He opened the bundle and showed me the equivalent of two handfuls of carrot ends and peelings.

"Well, let's give them to him."

I stepped aside and let Lalo pass. We went through the house and out the back door. Pedro perked up his long ears and poked his nose over the edge of his pen.

I said, "He's got big teeth, and those are small pieces. Let's put them in his dish."

"I'll get it." Lalo handed me the bundle and climbed into the pen.

Pedro stood looking at me in expectation. I noted the light-colored area around his eyes and on his muzzle, grey and light brown, that looked spectral grey at night.

"Here it is," said Lalo. He set the battered tin feed dish on the ground, took the bundle from me, and shook the contents into the dish. He stood back and said, "When can I ride him again?"

"Not today, Lalo. There are lots of serious things going on."

"My sister said he got him with just one shot. Is that right?"

"Yes, it is."

"And *la señorita* Palomar is going to make things clear."

"I don't know. None of that should be repeated until it comes to pass."

"And you and *el señor* Dunbar are coming for supper again."

"She invited us. We went to the bank with her."

"And we'll all sleep in the house of Doña Dolores?"

"I suppose so, if she asks us to. With good reason she feels safer that way."

"There are evil people. The fat one gave me a bad eye when I walked past."

"Stay away from him."

"He has his arm in a bandage."

"He can still do harm. So don't go near him. When you go back, don't cross the street here and walk down the main street. Go by way of the stable and down that street."

"What's wrong with it?"

"I tell you, Lalo, something bad is going to happen before things get better. And the fat one has no good intentions. So go the other way to Doña Dolores's house, and keep an eye out there. You did well yesterday."

Lalo gave his simple smile. "I want to go to Horace's café and buy some candy."

I heaved out a breath. "Oh, all right. But stay on that side of the street, by the barbershop and the café. And turn at the next corner. Don't go past the jail."

"Oh, the man with the star is not there. He went with Ted in the wagon. To the ranch, I think. To get the dead one."

"He'll be back, and there will be trouble of some kind with him and the fat one. So don't get in the way."

Lalo dipped his head back and forth as he smiled. "They're

angry about the one who got the bullet, aren't they?"

"That and more. Do you have money for candy?"

"La *señorita* Palomar gave me a *peseta.*"

That was his word for a two-bit piece. "Good," I said. "Just be careful, and go the way I told you."

Emilia served us a dinner of venison stew, and I was glad to see that the deer meat was holding out and not going to waste. The cool weather had been good for the meat I had left, as well.

Along with the stew, Emilia set out two plates of warm biscuits. Regina took a biscuit and cut it in half. After she spread some butter and closed the two halves, she said, "I don't think we should have any trouble getting an audience of at least three people, even on short notice. Do you?"

Dunbar said, "Do you plan to have a reading in the morning?"

"That's my idea."

After a few seconds of thought, I said, "Have you got a place in mind for this reading?"

"Nothing arranged, but Emilia mentioned a café."

"That would be good," I said. "It belongs to a friend of ours, Horace. Nothing is very far in this town, but it's right across the street from the bank. Very convenient, if you plan to get the letter then. I'll be happy to ask him."

Regina smiled, not quite in the way she had charmed Henry Lauck, but pleasant all the same. "Thank you," she said. "It will be a great help."

We spent the evening as we had the night before, with Dunbar and me perusing old newspapers while Regina busied herself in Dolores's office. At one point, Dunbar went in to visit with her for a while, but he did not stay long. When it came time to go to sleep, the women retired into their bedroom. Lalo, who had kept his sister company in the kitchen and had gone out from time to time to patrol the outside of the house, bedded down in the pantry. Dunbar and I went to our pallets in the spare room.

As we settled under our covers in the dark, I spoke across to him. "I have to admit I'm uneasy about what might happen tomorrow." I recalled Lalo's words from the day of Dolores's funeral. *Mala estrella.* Bad star.

"With good reason," said Dunbar.

"I'm glad Regina is taking the initiative, but the chances of something going wrong are too great."

Dunbar said, "Oh, you can bet something will go wrong. We'll just have to be ready for it."

I was having a dream about leading Pedro on a high mountain trail when I was blasted out of my sleep. The window panes rattled, and the house lumber creaked.

Dunbar and I were both sitting up. I heard him toss his blankets aside and begin to put on his boots.

"What was that?" I asked.

"It sounded like an explosion."

"From town?"

"I think so."

Voices and movement sounded from the other room. Dunbar called in that direction. "It's not here. I think it's in town. Be calm."

As I put on my boots, I began to shiver. I reached for my coat and found it. I put it on and hunched together to try to stop the shivering. I found my hat and put it on, then stood up and buttoned my coat. When I got to the front room, a lamp was lit on the sideboard, and the women were huddled in their housecoats. At the edge of the light, Lalo stood open-mouthed and silent.

Dunbar, already in his hat, coat, and boots, had opened the front door and was standing with his ear turned toward town.

He said, "I hear voices. Something's happened. We'd best go see."

I tensed my muscles and tried to shiver warmth into my upper body. I said, "I agree."

"We'll stay here," said Regina. "Unless you think otherwise."

Dunbar said, "Whatever it is, it's there and not here. I think you'll be all right." In Spanish he said, "Lalo, stay here and take care of these ladies."

With no further delay, we went out into the chilly night. As we walked along at a brisk pace, sounds came from all over town. When we reached the main street, I saw a group of people in the street in front of the bank. At least half a dozen lanterns were lit, and men were milling around, talking, calling out.

We walked down the middle of the street, and when we were less than half a block away, I distinguished forms from shadows and saw the first part of the damage. The upper half of the front wall of the bank was gone. Stones had fallen onto the sidewalk and into the street. Some men were inside the building, and several stood outside. Voices carried back and forth. Closer, I saw that the front door was hanging by a hinge. A man came out with a lantern, said something, and went back in.

Ted the barber was standing near the door. I asked him what had happened.

He said, "Robbery. Someone tried to blow the vault open."

No one was guarding the door, so Dunbar and I went in. A small group of men stood back by the vault with a couple of lanterns, and voices came from a little farther in. I looked around me. In the glow of the light, I could see that the service counter had been shattered. Splintered boards stuck up and out, and jagged splinters lay on the floor with fragments of rock.

The bars of the iron gate were mangled, and the heavy door of the vault sagged open. Lamplight in the passageway showed where the wall of safe-deposit boxes had been reduced to a pile of rubble and bits of metal. A man was poking at the mound with a long iron rod. Another was turning over the debris with a shovel.

The man with the rod turned and squinted into the lamplight, and the star on his vest reflected the glow. "The rest of you get out of here," he said. "A crime's been committed here." He turned to the man with the shovel. "Henry, get one of those lanterns and hold it for me. Everyone else get out."

A voice from behind me said, "Not me."

I turned to see Walter Eliot in a dark wool overcoat and a derby hat.

"Of course you can stay," said the marshal. "We just need to get these others out so we can look for evidence and see what the damage is."

Eliot said, "We'll need at least two lights." His eyes fell on Jim Sloane, who held the other lantern. "How about you?" he said.

"Any way I can help."

"Good," said Eliot. "Now I'll ask everyone else to leave." His eyes swept over us, not stopping on anyone. "Just get out. Please."

Dunbar and I went out to the street, where a crowd of twenty men had gathered. I did not know all of them. I imagined some had come from the saloon and some from the boarding house, and I guessed that every man in town except for Man Mountain Montgomery—and Lalo—was there. We found Horace, who was wearing his cap and jacket and looking none too happy.

"Shattered my front window," he said. "Sons of bitches."

Ben the store clerk said, "Lotta damage for the little bit of money they'd get out of it."

"Bah," said Horace. "Some people just don't care."

Voices quieted, and I turned to see two women approaching.

Emilia in a wool ulster was carrying a lamp, while Regina in her dark wool cloak walked alongside. When they came up to us, Regina said, "Lalo's curiosity got the better of him, so he ran off to see what happened. When he came back and told us what it was, we decided to come and see for ourselves."

"I'm afraid there's been a lot of damage," said Dunbar.

"I'd like to know how much. Can we go in?"

I said, "They want everyone to stay out. Ted's watching the door. I'll see if he can get Henry for you."

I went to the door and asked Ted to see if he could persuade Henry to come out for a minute. I offered to watch the door for him. I added, "And if you would, tell Henry that Miss Palomar is here. She's very worried."

A couple of minutes later, Henry came out. His forehead was smudged, and he had a discouraged look on his face. He said, "Miss Palomar, I'm sorry to say there's been a great deal of damage. The whole wall of safe-deposit boxes was blown apart, and everything is in fragments. I've looked especially for your things, but I haven't found anything that I could identify."

Regina heaved a sigh. "I'm sorry to hear that."

"I assure you I didn't pay undue attention, but, yes, I saw the size and nature of them, and I don't see anything like that in the rubble. I'm very sorry."

She sighed again. "So am I. But I'm sure the bank's losses are greater than mine." She raised her eyes to meet his. "Thank you so much for your attention."

"I wish I could do more."

"You've done more than I could ask for. Don't let me keep you any longer."

"Good night." He gave a slight bow and walked away.

Regina turned to Dunbar and me. "I'm not sure where that leaves us, but I think it would still be worthwhile to have a meeting in the morning."

I spoke up. "By the way, this is Horace." I motioned for him to step closer. "He has the café. Horace, this is Miss Regina Palomar. Dolores's sister."

"I knew her on sight." He smiled and nodded to her. "As beautiful as Dolores." His eyes blinked a couple of times, and he added, "I was a great admirer of your sister, if only at a distance."

Regina did not answer right away, so I said, "Miss Palomar would like to have a get-together in the morning, at about nine. What would you think of having it in the café?"

He said, "Fine with me. If you don't mind a broken window. I'll have things swept up and a full pot of coffee ready."

"Thank you," I said. As I thought of the next morning, the dread feeling I had had before, that something bad was going to happen, still clung to me. I also recalled, from earlier that evening, Dunbar's comment that something was bound to go wrong. As lamplight wavered and voices carried on the cold night air, I was sure that the bad thing had not happened with the blowing up of the bank. It was yet to come.

CHAPTER TWELVE

A light snow had begun to fall when Dunbar, Regina, and I set out for the Desert Rose Café the next morning. The small flakes were melting as they made contact, but I imagined that if the snow kept up, it would begin to accumulate as the day went along.

Horace had a blanket tacked up to cover the broken window. Inside, he had a lamp lit as well as a blaze going in the stove in the dining area, so the chill was off the air. Dunbar and I helped him move a couple of tables together and set eight chairs in place. The chairs were cold to the touch, but not bad. Horace scooted back the chair nearest the stove and told Regina she might like to sit there.

Ted the barber was first to arrive, then Ross Ferguson and his clerk, Ben. A couple of minutes later, Walter Eliot walked in. He was wearing the same derby hat and wool overcoat as the night before. He took off his hat, held it aside, and tapped it to shake off any snowflakes or moisture.

"I don't know what this portends," he said. "But if it has anything to do with the bank, I think the marshal should be here." He trained his spectacles on me, as if he didn't know Regina or Dunbar well enough to direct the question to either of them. "Does it?" he asked.

I said, "I'm not sure, but I think it might."

Eliot waved his hat. "Then he should be here. Ted, why don't you run down and get him. He said he was going to bunk in the jail. He was up late, sifting through all the damage, but so was I. And I'm here."

"Sure." Ted got up and went out into the snowy morning.

Horace came out of the kitchen with a coffeepot. "Where's Henry?"

Eliot spread the skirts of his coat and sat down. "Somebody had to stay with the building."

"All night?"

"He's been there."

"Should we send over some coffee or something warm to eat?"

"He can come over here after we're done."

Horace went to the counter and came back with eight cups. He set one in front of each chair. I counted the people. Already present were Regina, Horace, Dunbar, myself, Eliot, Ferguson, and Ben. Ted would be eight, and the marshal, if he came, would make nine.

I sat across the corner of the table from Regina on her right. Dunbar sat opposite me, on her left. Eliot sat at the other end, while Ferguson and Ben sat on either side of him.

Ted came in and said, "He'll be here in a minute." He looked around, and seeing his previous seat taken, he sat down between Ben and me.

Horace poured coffee for everyone at the table, then stood back by the counter. No one spoke for several long minutes until footsteps crunched outside.

Ted's cheerful voice bubbled up. "Sounds like him."

The door opened, and Pat Roderick came in. He was wearing a canvas coat that covered part of his star and reached to the handle of his six-gun. He had a day's stubble on his cheeks, and his eyes were a little bleary. He did not look at anyone as he took a place behind Eliot and Ferguson.

"Seat over here," said Horace, pointing at the chair next to Dunbar.

"I'll stand."

Eliot cleared his throat. "I think there's enough people here to get started."

My heartbeat picked up. My attention was divided in two directions between the marshal and Regina. I saw that Dunbar was keeping an eye on Roderick, so I found that assuring.

Regina's voice had a faint quaver as she began. "I have asked for this meeting in accordance with a wish of my late sister, Dolores Carreau."

I saw the marshal, looking downward, take a slow breath.

Regina continued. "She left a letter, and she expressed to me in separate correspondence as well as on the envelope of her sealed letter, a wish that it should be read in the presence of at least three people, in the event of her unexpected death."

Eliot spoke. "And was that letter in the deposit box that you looked into yesterday morning?"

"It was. I looked at the envelope itself, but I did not open it at that time."

A flush rose on Eliot's face, and his voice had an accusing tone. "Then that may have been the cause for someone setting off a bomb in my bank."

"It may have been, but fortunately I took the letter with me."

"Henry said you put it back in the box." Eliot swallowed, as if he realized he had said too much.

"Henry thought I did." Regina's voice was sweet. "But the light was dim, and Henry, though he was watching more than he needed to, was polite enough not to stare at what I was doing."

Eliot rose in his chair as he took a deep breath. "So you still have the letter."

"Yes, I do."

"And you caused my bank to be blown up for nothing?"

Horace cut in. "Oh, get off it, Walter. Whoever set that bomb had a motive. It's not this lady's fault."

Ross Ferguson intervened. "Let's get back to the subject at hand. Miss Palomar, do you have that letter with you?"

"I do."

Ferguson moved his head so that his heavy-lidded eyes took in everyone at the table. "Then I propose that you read it, and we listen."

"Very well." Regina reached into the folds of her cloak and took out an envelope with handwriting on it.

Horace had moved to stand behind the empty chair, apparently to hear better. I thought all eyes were on Regina, but Dunbar pushed back his chair and stood up as the marshal stepped forward with his gun drawn.

"You can give me that letter," he said.

Dunbar had his gun drawn as well. He stepped clear of Horace and said, "Not so fast."

"I want that letter."

"On whose authority?"

Roderick seemed to miss the echo. With a curt tone he said, "I'll need it for state's evidence."

"You mean to suppress evidence."

The marshal, nearly a head taller than Horace, wrapped his arm around the older man's neck and held his pistol to the grey temple. He said, "Now I'm not playing any games." No one moved at the table as Roderick stepped backward and took Horace with him. "I'll say it again. I want that letter. Ross, you tuck it in my coat pocket here, or I'm sorry to say you'll have blood all over you."

Horace said, "Don't give him a damn thing."

Regina shook her head. She handed me the envelope. I handed it to Ted, who reached across the table and gave it to

Ross Ferguson. He put it in Roderick's coat pocket and patted the flap down over it.

"Here's how it is," said the marshal. "No one leaves this town for an hour. If you do, any one of you, you won't see this old bird alive again. Open the door, Ben."

The store clerk opened the door and stepped aside. Roderick backed out of the café with his hostage and pulled the door closed. Footsteps sounded outside as the two of them headed in the direction of the jail.

A series of breaths and mutterings went around the table. The sound of footfalls from two or more horses and a carriage came from the street, and I wondered what someone would think of the marshal walking down the sidewalk with the café owner.

The door opened on its own, and a cold draft blew in. The marshal must not have pulled the door all the way shut.

Eliot said, "Close the door, Ben."

The clerk got up and did as he was told.

Eliot shook his head as he took in an audible breath through his nose. He directed his gaze at Regina and said, "Nothing good is coming of any of this. And as far as that goes, nothing good ever came of your sister living in this town, either."

Dunbar had holstered his gun and was still standing. He stepped over to Eliot's chair, and quick as a cat he grabbed the man by the coat, hauled him out of his chair, and slammed him against the wall. He said, "None of us came to hear that kind of talk. Keep it to yourself or to those who want to hear it." He let loose of the banker's coat and went back to stand behind his own chair.

Eliot stood by the door and smoothed his coat. He raised his chin and said, "I'd like to know what we're going to do, then."

Dunbar turned to Regina. "Do you have anything else for this meeting?"

Her face had paled, and her voice seemed less steady than before as she said, "Yes, I do." Reaching again into her cloak, she took out another envelope. "After I acquired the letter yesterday, I found time to make a fair copy of it. Originally, I had not planned even to take the letter. But when I saw how Henry was taking so much interest in what I was doing, I decided to take it with me, and once I did that, I thought it would be prudent to make a copy."

I felt as if I had the breath taken away from me, but in a good way. I had felt all along that Regina was as cultivated and capable as her sister but not made powerless by the past. Now I admired her. She had nerve as well as prudence. I didn't know if she had told Dunbar about the letter, but he did not seem surprised at what she said.

Ross Ferguson's eyes opened. "Oh, so you have a copy?"

"I have the original. I put the copy in the envelope that your marshal now has."

Eliot had taken his seat again. He said, "How do we know that?"

Regina gave him a steady look. "As much as you can know anything, I imagine. But the handwriting in this letter can be compared with any of several items in my sister's house."

"Well, let's hear it, then."

"I don't need your instruction. It's what I intended to do all along."

With that she took out the letter. Those of us around the table were as quiet as if we were gathered around a coffin. The papers rustled, and Regina began to read, bringing us a voice from beyond the grave.

My name is Dolores Carreau. I was born María Dolores Palomar, and I came to the town of Cantera to be the governess for the family of Pierre Carreau. He and his wife, Angélique, had a son, André, and they hoped to have more children.

190

But Angélique's health was frail, and the doctor advised that she not go through childbirth again. Still they tried, and she lost a baby through miscarriage. Her health declined from there, and she left this life as a very young woman. I stayed on to take care of André, and within a year I married Mr. Carreau and became the little boy's stepmother.

I write this much to give a broad outline of the circumstances under which the most terrible of things happened. I am speaking, of course, of the death of little André, for which I will be guilty until the end of my days and beyond.

A small commotion went around the other end of the table, with someone clearing his throat, someone muttering, and a couple of men shifting in their chairs. When the noise died down, Regina continued to read.

The trouble began before I married Mr. Carreau, and even before the death of his first wife. I was a young woman, educated and from a respectable family, and in men's eyes, at least, not unattractive. I had my share of admirers, some more covert than others. One was Tim Sexton, who worked in a local business and who was openly fond of me. Another was Mr. Carreau himself, even before the decline and death of his wife. And another was Pat Roderick, whose name I never say and can barely force myself to write. For the sake of truth I spell it out, but for the rest of this account I will refer to him only as "R."

From the beginning of his attentions to me, this man seemed to have a power over me that I could not repel. It was something in his bearing that I could not understand until I learned that he was a peeping Tom. He began his play for me with insinuations, but before long he let me know more directly that he had observed some things that transpired between Mr. Carreau and myself.

Mr. Carreau, as I stated above, showed interest in me. As I

191

would come to find out, I was not the only one. At any rate, he was forward with me early on. I resisted, but he was importunate. To my shame I will admit here that I acceded to him when his wife was in her latter stage. I could say that he imposed himself upon me, but it is fairer to say that he was insistent and I acceded, and more than once. This man R. spied on us on at least two occasions, and when he came to me, he threatened to tell Mrs. Carreau unless I gave in to him.

I believe it was here that I first felt the power he was able to exert over me. He gloated over having seen me in a compromising situation, and in my feeling so vulnerable and exposed, it was as if he had already possessed me in that way. Moreover, I cannot deny that whatever weakness, or even desire, that allowed me to give in to Mr. Carreau also allowed me to do so here. But it was more than just a weakness of sin. Having thought through this at length, I realize I had a sense of having betrayed Mrs. Carreau with her husband; and then, as if to balance things out, one betrayal with another, I gave in to this other man. He mastered the opportunity, and I cannot express with what demonic pleasure he seemed to take his prize.

Meanwhile, I thought Tim Sexton had some idea of what was going on, and R. must have thought so, too. He developed quite a resentment toward Tim Sexton, which he expressed to me. Mr. Carreau, who was jealous and possessive, also formed a dislike for Tim, though he knew that in the public eye, there was no reason Tim could not pay his attentions to me.

If there was anything good in any of this, it was brought about by the death of Mrs. Carreau. When R. came around again, I was able to deny him. When he threatened to tell the Frenchman, as he called him, I told him Mr. Carreau would have his job. That cooled his ardor for a while, but he did not quit.

I married Mr. Carreau partly to keep this other man at bay and partly, I must admit, for the motive with which the public credited me, that being the desire for social position and financial security. Tim Sexton begged me not to, for my own sake if not his, and he was disconsolate when I did. R., on the other hand, seemed to think that my change in situation gave him new opportunity. He came around when Pierre was at the quarry, but I was able to keep him at a distance.

One day, which would become the worst day of my life, he came in the back door when I was in the kitchen. He began to make free with touching me, and I asked him to leave me alone. He said I knew what he had come for, that I had raised the Adam in him, and indeed he seemed to have his blood up.

While we were arguing, André came into the kitchen. He spoke good English as well as French, and he knew who R. was. He told the man he was going to tell his papa. R. said, "Get lost," and André said, in a louder voice, "I'm going to tell my papa. He says you're not worth a fig."

R. went into a rage. He grabbed André and shook him, and as the boy began to holler, R. grabbed the child's throat between his thumb and fingers and pinched him until he was silent. The body went limp, and R. dropped him to the floor. He turned to me, transfixed me with his burning eyes and pointing finger, and said, "If you ever breathe a word of this, I'll do the same to you."

He wrapped the little boy in a blanket and left with him. From that day forward I never spoke a word to that man. But I could not speak to anyone about what had happened. I was helpless, powerless. For a thousand times in the days and weeks that followed, I wished I could tell what I knew, but every day that passed made it harder, and my sense of complicity lay on me like an incubus.

This man would not have come around if I had not given him reason at some point, so I felt that it was my fault he had come there that day and in a worked-up state. Also, it was, or has been, in my nature to take on guilt. He knew me well enough to know that, and it was in his nature to shift the burden of guilt to his advantage. So in a strange way, this man still had the power to keep me silent, even though I had the power of knowledge over him. It was an unspoken truce, supported, I believe, by fear and hatred on my side and self-assured mastery on his.

The rest of the story is well known, or mostly so. The blame fell on Tim Sexton, and Pierre was all for it. R. found a man, one Dade Flynn, who was willing to say he saw Tim accost the boy near the trough where the body was found, and that was enough. I knew the testimony was false, of course, but I could not summon up the fortitude to come forward and disprove it.

So Tim went to prison, unjustly, and time went on. Pierre's business went bad, and his health did as well. He died of apoplexy, the result of anger, grief, and despair that built up within him. He blamed me for the death of his son, though he never had a specific reason why. Moreover, he did not consider me to be his family, as I was not his first wife, let alone a blood relation, so he left me a small allotment, to be canceled if I were to re-marry. Most of his property he entailed to other heirs.

During his life, he always maintained that he was missing sums of money. When the heirs came, they suspected me of embezzling it, but the losses went back to a time before Pierre knew me. Then they discovered that he had a mistress, and a son, that he had maintained since his earlier life in Louisiana. Even as late as his marriage to me, he would see this other woman, Monique, when he went on trips.

I have reason to believe that the natural son was Philip Gaston. Shortly before he was found dead at the quarry, he came to see me. He seemed quite interested in knowing how An-dré had died. I do not know if it was curiosity on his part, as

André would have been his half-brother, or whether it might have something to do with his hopes to augment his own expectations. Whatever the case, I decided to write this letter when his body was found at the Celeste. Still I delayed, until Tim Sexton came back to town and met his end. Then I thought that the old, silent balance might be thrown off, and I wanted to put in my word while I could.

People will believe as they wish. For my part, I have prayed thousands of times for forgiveness. In this life I can never make things up to Angélique, Pierre, or André. But I can tell the truth here, even if I am the only one who ever reads it. To this I set my hand, Dolores Carreau, on the fifth day of October, in the year of our Lord eighteen hundred and ninety-six.

The papers rustled as Regina evened them into a small stack. Breathing and muttering went around the table as before.

"By Jove," said Eliot. "And to think I've been living in the Frenchman's house all that time. And here she was, living down the street, and knew all about it."

I said, "Not to mention the man who has upheld the law for you all this time as well."

Eliot raised his eyebrows. "I wonder how much of it is true. Most of it, I guess, or he wouldn't have been so eager to get his hands on that letter." He took in a breath through his nose and said, "And I told him everything he ever wanted to know." Eliot looked around the table. "Well, what do we do next? I'd say we send for a sheriff."

Dunbar spoke up. "We might not be done here."

Ross Ferguson's heavy eyelids went up. "Does anyone have anything to add?"

After the others answered in the negative, Dunbar spoke again. "I've got a couple of things. One is that when I first inquired into Philip Gaston, I was told he was not a relative of Pierre Carreau. Since then, I have received a confirmation that he was indeed the natural son of Pierre Carreau but not one of his assigned heirs."

Eliot cut in. "What are you, some kind of Pinkerton man?"

"I'm a cowpuncher by trade. But I do this sort of thing as well. When I do, I work on my own. I've followed this case off and on, along with others, for several years. I came here on the occasion of Tim Sexton being released from prison. A while after my first inquiries about young Gaston, I learned that he was petitioning for a share of Carreau's estate. He was interested in another provision of Carreau's will, which was that if it were ever proven that the widow Carreau had a hand in the death of the boy, her limited allowance would be reverted to the other heirs, which he hoped would include himself."

Eliot's voice was impatient as he spoke again. "That's one. What's the other?"

"It's about Tim Sexton. I had an inkling that he was the stranger who came to town, but I waited too long to see what he would do. That was my mistake. Everyone knows he came to clear his name—"

"We don't *know* that," said Eliot.

"You should be a lawyer. Anyway, I'll put it this way. He made it known that he was going to come back to clear his name, and when it was known who he was, many people believed he had come back for that reason." Dunbar paused. "I, for one, was convinced of it. In the course of my work, as I have followed this case, I have never known of anyone seeing Dade Flynn after he left town."

Dunbar looked around to see that he had everyone's attention, and he continued. "I even heard one statement, in the form of a suspicion, that Dade Flynn never made it out of this town alive. I also have heard that not long after Flynn's disappearance, the marshal tried to buy an abandoned saloon, which was just a few doors down from the jail, but one of the other saloon owners bought it and moved his business there, leaving the other building vacant."

"That would be the Diamond," I said. "It was abandoned for a while."

"That's right." Dunbar looked around the table. "I believe the marshal would have had more interest in the property itself than in the saloon business."

"And what interest would that be?" asked Eliot.

Dunbar said, "He might have had an interest in it because it had a cellar, where, when it was abandoned, something got buried."

A murmur passed between Ferguson and Eliot. When it subsided, Dunbar spoke again. "If the body is still there, or the skeleton, it should be identifiable. Flynn had one silver tooth and silver linings on several others."

Eliot said, "That sounds like a fish story, or Long John Silver the pirate."

"Maybe it is. I don't expect anyone to believe it just from hearing it. But with a little digging, and the permission of Jim Sloane, you might find proof. I believe it's there, and like other things, it's been there all along."

Ross Ferguson blinked his heavy eyelids. "I wasn't here then, but it doesn't sound impossible."

Eliot's voice came up. "We still haven't answered my earlier question. What do we do next?"

"You can do what you want," said Dunbar. He nodded toward Ross Ferguson. "Maybe someone will talk to Jim Sloane. As for me, I'm going after Horace."

Eliot said, "I don't think the hour's up yet."

Dunbar gave him an indulgent look. "It'll take us a few minutes to get our horses ready. And we'll ride slow."

"I think we should send for a sheriff."

Dunbar now gave him a cold stare. "Time's a-wasting, and

this man wants to get away. We can't let that happen. No one expects you to go."

"I didn't mean—"

Dunbar dropped his hand flat on the table. "Here's what we've got. First off, a little boy was killed long ago, and the man who did it hasn't been held accountable. Instead, another man was falsely accused and then wrongly killed. In addition, a woman has lived in guilt and agony and silence—granted, some of it was brought about by her own doing, but fear kept her silent, and she died when discovery drew closer. And the man behind it all doesn't care how much damage is done or who gets hurt. He just wants to beat the game and be exempt from justice. We can't let him get away with it."

"Of course," said Eliot. "But I don't want to see another innocent person get hurt. Give Roderick time, and he'll leave Horace alone."

"You can stay here if you want. But I'm not going to sit around and wait to see what happens."

CHAPTER THIRTEEN

The light snow was still falling. It was beginning to accumulate on the ridges of ruts in the street and on weeds that grew here and there on the way to the livery stable.

I said to Dunbar, "What about this story about Dade Flynn? You said all the dead people were accounted for."

"Well, I don't know for sure that he's dead. It's just a good hunch. When I made that comment, what I meant was, there aren't any missing bodies. Not anyone who was known to have gone missing. And we were talking about the Bluestone Quarry. I still don't think there are any there, unless the marshal has other skeletons. Which he may have, but if he does, he acquired it after all this other business."

At the livery stable, Jess Fluornoy stood by as Dunbar brushed the blue roan. Both the roan and the buckskin had been in a pen outside, and their backs and sides were streaked with moisture from the melted snow. The stable man did not speak, but he had an air of interest about him.

Glancing aside from his work, Dunbar asked, "How did the marshal leave town?"

"Sort of in a hurry."

"On a horse? By himself?"

"He had me saddle three horses while he went for his hired man."

"Montgomery."

"The only one he's got left."

"Then I guess the hired hand's arm doesn't hurt him too much to ride."

"Seemed that way."

"Then they left together?"

"The hired man came for the horses and went downtown, and a little while later I heard horses riding west of town. I guess it was them. I thought the whole thing was curious. But Roderick's the marshal and I'm not."

"I think he would agree with you on that. By the way, what time was this?"

"The marshal was here at about nine, and his man showed up about ten minutes later."

When Dunbar had the horses saddled, we led them out and mounted up. I caught his eye and said, "What do you think?"

"Looks like the marshal had a plan ready if he needed it. And he did."

We stopped at my place long enough for Dunbar to go in and get his rifle. I held the horses as he tied on the scabbard. All the while, I debated on whether to bring a gun myself. I decided I would, so I went into the house and dug out an old .38 revolver I had not fired in years. It had five cartridges in the cylinder. I could not find any more, so I stowed the gun in my coat pocket and went out to join Dunbar.

Heading west from town, we found the trail easy to follow. The horse hooves and wagon wheel rims had pressed the light snow into the grass and had lifted bits of damp soil. Our horses moved at a fast walk for about half a mile until Dunbar put us into a lope.

I have heard about men galloping fifty miles across country, but even a couple of miles was hard work for me. Snowflakes hit me in the face and stung my bare eyes as I clutched the saddle horn and tried to keep my seat. When I turned my head down against the onrush of air, I saw the snow and grass and earth flowing beneath me. I was breathing hard. Every few seconds I would look up to be sure I was on course, and the snowflakes would hit me again. In addition to stinging my eyes, they hung on my eyelashes, melted on my lips and tongue, and ran down my cheeks as if I were crying. Ahead of me, Dunbar rode smooth and steady, leaning into the wind and the weather. Snow was gathering on the brim and crown of his dark hat. He turned to check on me, nodded, and bent again to his purpose.

Just as I was wondering how much longer I could hold on, Dunbar slowed his horse to a walk. The buckskin slowed down as well, jolting me as he changed gaits. As we kept going, I settled into my seat and pulled myself together. The wind created by our fast riding had diminished. I wiped my eyes and rubbed my nose, then felt for the pistol to make sure it was still there.

The horses were sending out clouds from their heavy breathing, but they stepped along at a good pace. Dunbar held his reins with one hand as he brushed his mustache with the other.

He said, "Good thing we didn't bring the banker along. I don't think he'd be half the rider you are."

"Then he wouldn't be much."

"Oh, you're doin' fine. And it's not that far."

Two more medleys of loping and walking brought us to a low hill within a quarter-mile of the ranch house. Dunbar drew rein and said, "We need to take it slow from here. We don't know what to expect. We may have to split up."

We dismounted, and I held the horses as Dunbar bent over and walked up the slope of the hill. Near the crest, he took off his hat and raised his head little by little. He took out his small pair of binoculars, looked for a minute, and turned away. He put on his hat as he came back down the hill.

He handed me the binoculars and said, "Go take a look, and come right back."

Leaning forward, I walked to the top of the hill and knelt. The ranch yard lay to the northwest. I raised the binoculars and focused the view. It didn't make sense at first. Across the dirt yard from the house sat a shed, which was all the ranch had by way of a barn. Half of it was an open wagon shed, facing south. A one-horse buggy was backed partway into it, with the horse still harnessed and standing in the light falling snow. Man Mountain Montgomery was standing just inside the shed, holding the coils of a rope and tossing up the loose end. I saw that he was trying to throw the rope through the space between the roof and the front crossbeam that supported the rafters. Moving the binoculars, I saw Horace a yard or so inside the shed. He was standing up straight with his hands in back of him, so I assumed he was tied. Worse, he had a rope around his neck. It went down to the ground and up again into the hands of Man Mountain Montgomery. Then I realized that Montgomery no longer had his arm in a sling.

I hurried down the hill and handed the binoculars to Dunbar. I said, "They can't be thinking of—"

"My guess is that the marshal is already gone, and this is their way of buying time. But we can't take chances. He's going to put Horace up onto the back of that buggy. So here's my idea. I'll ride up there in plain view. In the meanwhile, you go around in back, and when things break loose, you lay your hands on that buggy horse for all you're worth."

"I don't know if I can hold a horse if someone fires a shot."

"I'll try not to, but we don't know."

I took in a deep breath. "All right. I'll give it a try." He gave me the reins to the buckskin. I positioned the horse so I was standing uphill, and with another big breath I stuck my boot in the stirrup and pulled myself aboard. My leg muscles felt weak, but I caught my other stirrup and set off.

I kept to low ground as I rode north. A couple of times I

moved uphill to take a look, and when I was sure I was out of view from the front of the shed, I turned west into open country and rode around wide of the shed and came in on the blind side. I dismounted and, knowing that Dunbar had the buckskin trained to stay put, I dropped the reins on the ground.

I took the .38 from my pocket, then put it back as I realized I would need both hands to hang onto that horse. Just as I got to the corner of the shed, I heard Man Mountain Montgomery's deep voice.

"Get back, you son of a bitch."

Peeking around, I saw that the buggy horse had walked about five yards out from the shed. Montgomery was pushing with his left shoulder and reaching across with his right hand to pull on the leather cheek piece. The horse, a husky dark brown animal, was throwing his head back.

I took out my pistol again. At that point, the brown horse whickered. Montgomery eased up and looked around, away from me. I had to lean out further to see beyond the horse and the man, and as I did, I saw Dunbar riding in. He was over a hundred yards away, but he had his pistol drawn.

Montgomery left the horse alone and walked back into the shed. The buggy was far enough ahead that I could see him. He pulled on one of the two lengths of rope coming down from the beam, and the other part wiggled up, slithered over the beam like a snake, and dropped in a loose heap on the ground. Montgomery grabbed the upper end of the rope a couple of feet from Horace's neck and hauled the old man into the open.

"Don't move," he said

Dunbar was fifty or sixty yards away and riding in at a walk. He had put his gun in his holster.

Montgomery called out, "Throw your gun in the dirt, Mister Snoop, or something bad could happen to this old man."

I wondered how much Montgomery was bluffing. I didn't

know if he had it in him to hang a man, but I was convinced he was hoping to use his hostage to get at Dunbar by himself, in the open, miles from town. He and Roderick had no doubt counted on not having much of a posse, and as far as Montgomery could see, Dunbar was alone, just as the big man would have wanted. Furthermore, Montgomery had a bloated enough opinion of himself that he would think he could finish off Dunbar and get away.

Dunbar had both hands on his saddle horn as he kept riding in. He called back. "It's your choice whether you want to get out of here on your own two feet or go like your pal Lee Porter did."

"Don't scare me." Montgomery cocked the pistol, and Dunbar stopped the horse about forty yards away. The big man said, "You know, I'm not surprised that none of the other fine citizens came out with you. Not a lot of courage in that bunch." With his left hand on the rope, he drew his gun with his right hand and poked the barrel into Horace's neck. He cleared his throat and called out, "So throw your gun in the dirt like I said."

Dunbar did not move. Everything seemed to hang in the air for one long second and another.

Montgomery's voice cut the air again. "Throw down your gun!"

Dunbar sat with his hands on the pommel and his horse backed up a step.

"Son of a bitch!" Montgomery pointed his gun in Dunbar's direction and fired, but as he did, Horace stomped on his foot. Dirt and snow kicked up to the left of Montgomery's aim. The buggy horse bolted. Dunbar's horse reared up and wheezed, and Dunbar slid off.

Montgomery tried to pick up his target as Dunbar stumbled to gain his footing. I held my .38 up with both hands, but I was shaking, and Horace was not well enough out of my line of fire. As I was bearing down, another two guns blasted, not a second apart. Man Mountain Montgomery raised his pistol as he turned, then let it drop as he staggered back once, twice, and fell to the ground. Dunbar kept his pistol aimed as he moved forward. The blue roan had settled down and stood a few yards back.

I came out of my place of concealment. Dunbar stood in silence, his hand resting on his pistol butt, as he eyed the body on the ground. Horace was standing with his chin raised. I walked over to him and took the rope from his neck, then began working on the knots that held his hands tied.

He said, "Thanks. I didn't like that rope at all around my neck."

Dunbar came over and stood next to us. "Where's Roderick?" he asked.

Horace moved his head. "He went that way. To the quarry."

"How long ago did he leave?"

"About fifteen minutes ago. He took awhile getting things together."

"Did he take just one horse?"

"Yeh. He tied a duffle bag on back. And he's got a rifle, too." Horace coughed.

Dunbar said, "Thanks. I'm goin' after him. Owen, are you still in?"

"I'd better be." I looked Horace over. He had snow on his hair and on his jacket, his shoulders sagged, and he had a tired expression on his face. "Are you all right?" I asked.

"Oh, I'm fine. A hell of a lot better than I was ten minutes ago."

"If you want, then, you can take this buggy back to town. I don't think anyone's in a position to complain."

"Sure. That's all right with me. I didn't care for the horseback ride out here. Anything you want me to say when I get to town?"

I said, "You might ask Ted to do the marshal one last favor and haul this one off to be buried. I don't know what else is going to happen, but we can't just leave him here."

Horace gave the body a look of contempt. "It wouldn't hurt my feelings to leave him here to rot. But I'm not a good Christian like you are."

"That's two people I outshine today." I patted Horace on the shoulder and brushed off a skiff of snow. "I'll see you soon."

"I hope so."

Dunbar and I mounted up, and with Dunbar in the lead we followed the marshal's tracks through the light snow. We left the ranch yard, rode past the skeletal house of stone, and entered the canyon of Bluestone Quarry. Thin layers of snow covered the rocks wherever they jutted up, and an uneven blanket of white lay on the ground. The trail was easy to follow with the snow and the particles of sandstone dug up by the fast-moving hooves. If Roderick had turned off to hide behind a rock formation it would have been obvious, but the tracks led straight ahead.

We rode through the canyon for half a mile, farther than I had been before, until we came to a natural gate where two sandstone walls came within six feet of one another. We dismounted and walked forward. Beyond the opening, the canyon widened again into a large bowl, oval-shaped, perhaps a hundred yards across and two hundred yards long. The rock walls were yellow, the slopes were white with snow, and the empty middle was a yawning black hole. The pit.

The left side came down sheer and then sloped, with nothing like a ledge or shelf. On the right side, a narrow ledge ran halfway around, uphill and then down, and ended at a crevice on the other side of the big hole. The dark cleft was just wide enough to be the passageway I had told Dunbar about.

A hundred and fifty yards away, on a diagonal across the empty space, a man was yanking on the reins and trying to pull a horse up the path. It was one of those ledges that was wide enough to be a game trail but too narrow for a man to want to be on horseback. The width of his leg would push the horse too far from the wall. The marshal's predicament was evident. The duffle bag on the back of the saddle was hanging up on the rock. There was no way he could get to it to untie it unless he could back the horse all the way around, which would be tricky in itself, and he needed to go forward to get to the crevice. From there, he could hold off any pursuers who dared to go around on the ledge and, once inside, he could follow the canyon through the rock. But right now he was stuck. He had had one good thought, though, and that was to pull the rifle from the scabbard before he started out ahead of the horse. Now he was holding the rifle with one hand and pulling on the reins with the other, as the horse balked at the canvas bag rubbing against the rock wall.

Dunbar gave me his reins and drew his rifle out of the scabbard. I moved our horses so that they were off to the side of the gateway in the rock.

Dunbar went forward, holding the rifle at waist level, and called across the cold distance. "Roderick!"

The marshal turned and stared.

"Roderick! You might as well give up!"

"Go to hell."

"It's all up, Roderick. Everyone knows. They'll get you one way or another."

Roderick shifted his rifle to his left hand where he held the reins. With his right, he drew his pistol and fired. The bullet pinged away, and the shot echoed. Meanwhile, the horse pulled back and bunched its feet. I could see its nostrils widen even at that distance. Roderick holstered his pistol and transferred the rifle to his right hand. With his left, he jerked the reins again.

The horse came forward, the duffle bag caught on the rock, and the horse pulled back. A foot slipped, came back up. The horse shifted its feet, then another one slipped, and the horse made frantic stabs as its feet went out from under it. With a wheeze and a grunt it slipped over the edge, turned, hit the sloping wall, and fell out of sight. A thud and a splashing sound rose from the pit together, and the horse began to squeal. Roderick was leaned back against the wall, taking deep breaths.

Dunbar put his cupped hand to his mouth. "Throw your guns down in there, and come out on your own."

Roderick moved his head up and around, as if he had a sore neck. The horse was still squealing. Roderick moved his head back in the other direction, then took a full breath. The horse was quiet for a second, and when it began to squeal again, Roderick aimed his rifle into the pit and fired. The shot made a muted, hollow sound, and the horse went quiet.

Roderick held the rifle at waist level as he spoke in a loud voice but not quite a holler. "Come and get me." Then he turned and began walking along the ledge toward the crevice at the far end of the pit.

Dunbar raised his rifle and fired. Chips flew from the rock wall in front of Roderick. The man stopped, raised his rifle, and fired back. Dunbar dropped to the ground, and the bullet split the air as it passed through the gateway. Roderick levered in another shell, aimed, pulled the trigger, and started to walk again.

Dunbar raised to a crouch and fired like before at the rock wall in front of the man. Roderick hollered, "Then take this, you son of a bitch!" He fired his rifle one shot after another, three times together, until Dunbar took aim at the man himself and hit him dead center. Roderick's coat was unbuttoned, and the star on his vest flashed as he stepped forward, dropped his rifle, and followed it into the abyss.

★ ★ ★ ★ ★

A small crowd had gathered in the Diamond Saloon when Dunbar and I got back to town. Half a dozen men sat in a semicircle around two small tables pushed together. Facing this arrangement was a small table by itself with no chairs around it but a pale object sitting in the center. As my eyes adjusted to the dim light, I saw that the object was a human skull. The eye sockets were dark but not ghoulish. A few bits of dry integuments stuck to the bone, which was uneven in its discoloration and deteriorating across the nose area. But most of the teeth were intact, including one silver tooth and several dull white ones with silver linings.

I counted the men around the table and recognized each one: Ted, Jess Fluornoy, Ben, Horace, Jim Sloane, and Ross Ferguson.

"Is that Dade Flynn?" I asked.

"Present but not voting," said Horace.

Fluornoy said, "Very much as I remember him, at least the teeth."

Jim Sloane cleared his throat. "And to think he'd been down there all this time."

Ben, who had been taking a sip of whiskey, set down his glass and said, "I guess that's what he gets for bearing false testimony."

Ross Ferguson said, "You weren't here then, and neither was I."

"That's true. And everyone makes mistakes."

Horace spoke again. "Well, I was here then, and I was here when Roderick pulled his last stunt. So I don't feel bad lookin' at this fellow now."

Everyone turned to gaze at the skull. I thought, he might have lied then, and he might be present but not voting now, but his presence itself was like another voice from beyond the grave.

CHAPTER FOURTEEN

Dunbar had the blue roan saddled and the buckskin packed by the time I finished cleaning up the kitchen the next morning. He had paid for his lodging after breakfast, so this was the moment of leave-taking.

We stood in the street in front of my place. An inch of snow lay on the ground, and the air was cold and still. Dunbar had his canvas coat buttoned halfway up, where a turquoise neck scarf was tucked into his charcoal-grey vest. As he took off his right glove to shake hands, I saw the spot in his palm. I was sure he saw me notice it, for he missed nothing, but as usual he paid it no attention.

His eyes held me in a friendly expression as he shook my hand and said, "So long, Owen. May your days be many."

"So long to you, Dunbar. I assume you said goodbye to Regina?"

He smiled as he put on his glove. "Oh, yes. I wouldn't have missed it."

"If you're ever back this way, be sure to drop in."

"I'll do that." His eyes went away and came back. "Take care of Emilia. And Lalo, too. And Pedro."

He got the saddle horse into position, set his reins, held the lead rope in one hand, and pulled himself aboard with the other. He touched the brim of his hat and snugged it, then gave me a final wave as he touched a spur to the blue roan. The buckskin with the canvas packs fell into line. Eight hooves clopped as

Dunbar rode away, a man with all the air of having things to tend to. He rode west a short way to the edge of town and turned north.

I went into the house, put on my hat and coat and gloves, and went out the back door. I put the halter on Pedro and led him down the alley and into the open. Dunbar was almost a mile away, riding north across the snowy plain toward the pine ridge where I had seen him that first day when he came down out of the mists. Although he said he might come back, I didn't expect to see him again in this barren land.

The seasons have come around three times since I last saw Dunbar, and the town of Cantera does not look much different than before. Horace still runs the Desert Rose Café, and Ted waves from his barber's chair. Jim Sloane still has the Diamond Saloon, where every now and then a range rider comes in who has not heard the story of Silver Tooth, the guest on the shelf.

Henry Lauck left town, having displeased his boss and wanting to find better domestic prospects anyway. Ben the clerk put in for the job of town marshal, but they gave it to Jum Bailey, who broke his ankle when he was thrown from a horse. He can't ride fast horses any more, but he keeps a gentle one at Jess Fluornoy's stable, and he limps well enough to make the rounds.

A couple of other small things have happened that didn't change the overall appearance of the town. In settling her sister's affairs, Regina saw that Dolores had left a small sum of money to Emilia, so it was not a hardship for Emilia not to have a house or a lady to look after. She still takes in laundry and ironing, but she does it at the lodging house. Combining our households has worked out well. Lalo does not have to go so far to give old tortillas to Pedro, Emilia serves much better meals than I did, and I have found time to work with my hands. With the lumber from Emilia's house and a few stones of my own gathering for a foundation, I have added a couple of rooms onto our establishment.

Walter Eliot brought the Bluestone Quarry back into operation for a short while. He hired two quarrymen, a freight wagon, and two stone masons and thus repaired his bank. He did not pay for the stone, for he turned right around and foreclosed on the ranch and quarry together. Not long after he took possession, he hired a dynamiter from Butte to slough away the canyon walls so that the rubble slid down and filled the pit. He said he did it as a safety measure, and perhaps he did. It also put a stop to Ted the barber taking curious sightseers out there on paid excursions. The place is for sale, but it's not going fast. If Eliot were to lower the price, though, it might offer an opportunity for someone whose wants were small and who would like to try his hand at making a living with a harvest of stones.

ABOUT THE AUTHOR

John D. Nesbitt lives in the plains country of Wyoming, where he teaches English and Spanish at Eastern Wyoming College. He writes western, contemporary, mystery, and retro/noir fiction as well as nonfiction and poetry. John has won many awards for his work, including two awards from the Wyoming State Historical Society (for fiction), two awards from Wyoming Writers for encouragement of other writers and service to the organization, two Wyoming Arts Council literary fellowships (one for fiction, one for nonfiction), and three Spur awards from Western Writers of America. His most recent books are *Dark Prairie* and *Don't Be a Stranger,* frontier mystery novels with Five Star.